MADELINE CAIN: THE ADVENTURE BEGINS

MADELINE CAIN: THE ADVENTURE BEGINS

EMILY CRAVEN

Craven Publishing

Brisbane

Dedication

To all the girlfriends in my life:

Gemma & Laani,

Emma, Johanna, Yujia, Sophie, Noni, Izzie, Lily & Kathy,

Maureen, Christine, Lauren, Carley, Aimee & Jodi

Nati & Sasha

Bridget, Mary Margaret & Vanessa;

You are smart, you are curious, you are brave.

Welcome!

Reader, you are currently one of my favourite people right now.

The Grand Adventures of Madeline Cain Series came out of a complete obsession with social media and Facebook specifically. I got all of the initial ideas for the (original) book one, The Grand Adventures of Madeline Cain, by setting up a Facebook event and inviting friends and family to fling all of their wildest ideas at me. At first it was a challenge to incorporate everything into the storyline, then it became just plain, laughter-inducing fun.

But the adventure felt incomplete without a genesis volume, one in which you discover where Madeline came from and what drove her out into the big wide world. This novella, the sequel to the series, tells that story. I hope you enjoy.

To your adventure!!

Madeline Cain: The Adventure Begins

Madeline Cain [+1 Add Friend]

*Goes to school at **Marryatville High School.** *Lives in **Adelaide, South Australia.** *Born on 07 November 1993.

Madeline Cain and **Kathy Bloomingdale** are now friends. [Add Kathy as a friend]

Madeline Cain and **Tim Gleeve** are now friends. [Add Tim as a friend]

10 more similar stories.

Madeline Cain joined the group **Melbourne Is A Backwater, But Adelaide's A City With Balls!** [Like . Join]

> **Kathy Bloomingdale** Seriously? The first thing you do when you create a Facebook profile is not tearfully announce you'll miss me or declare your undying friendship, but to like *that* page? Genital puns, that's how you're starting your online life? Shame on you, Madeline Cain, shame. *Posted Tuesday 6th September at 15:50* [Comment . Like]

> **Madeline Cain** Merely reminding you why Adelaide is the bomb. I was looking for one that referred to Ireland as a backwater, but this will have to do. *Posted Tuesday 6th September at 15:52* [Comment . Like]

> **Kathy Bloomingdale** *Tap tap tap tap* *Posted Tuesday 6th September at 15:52* [Comment . Like]

> **Madeline Cain** Fine, yes, I'm purposely missing the point. Is this

any better? *Posted Tuesday 6th September at 15:53* [Comment . Like]

Madeline Cain and **Mike Cain** are now friends. [Add Mike as a friend]

Madeline Cain When I told you I was normal, I may have exaggerated. *Posted Tuesday 6th September at 15:55* [Comment . Like]

> **Kathy Bloomingdale** Still not a declaration of eternal sisterhood, but ten points for accuracy ? *Posted Tuesday 6th September at 15:57* [Comment . Like]

> **Mike Cain** According to the dictionary, exaggeration indicates 'a stretching of the truth'. But that was a flat out Pinocchio. You're about as normal as an elephant doing the tango with a penguin. *Posted Tuesday 6th September at 15:59* [Comment . Like]

> **Madeline Cain** Brother dearest, if I'm *that* abnormal you have eight arms and tentacles coming out your eyeballs. Now kindly stop littering my Facebook profile with your unique brand of special. *Posted Tuesday 6th September at 16:02* [Comment . Like]

> **Kathy Bloomingdale** If you're lucky enough to find a weirdo, never let them go! *Posted Tuesday 6th September at 16:05* [Comment . Like]

> **Madeline Cain** I love you to, Kathy. I was just waiting for you to say it first ? *Posted Tuesday 6th September at 16:06* [Comment . Like]

Kathy Bloomingdale I want you all to know I love each and every one of you, though some more than others. Is that fair? No, but that's the situation we find ourselves in. *Posted Tuesday 6th September at 17:00* [Comment . Like]

> **Tim Gleeve** I will self-assign myself to the highest grade of love,

just to save you the hassle. *Posted Tuesday 6th September at 17:07* [Comment . Like]

Madeline Cain Our local narcissist, always looking out for others... *Posted Tuesday 6th September at 17:12* [Comment . Like]

Tim Gleeve What can I say, it's my gift and my cross to bear. But now I shall bare it in public, on my Book of the Face. Ultimately, it's your fault I've been set loose on social media, Maddie. *Posted Tuesday 6th September at 17:13* [Comment . Like]

Madeline Cain Not my fault! It's Kathy's! She's the one who's running away to Ireland for six weeks. How else are we supposed to keep in touch *and* save Kathy a million emails? *Posted Tuesday 6th September at 17:15* [Comment . Like]

Tim Gleeve You're right, let's blame Kathy. That curly hair wench who's abandoning us to go gallivanting with leprechauns. And now she's sending us blanket love, after all the sign up emails we waded through to get here. *Posted Tuesday 6th September at 17:18* [Comment . Like]

Kathy Bloomingdale You're just fuming because I figured out a way to circumnavigate my year twelve assessment *and* get entry into University twelve weeks early. Thank you STAT test! *Posted Tuesday 6th September at 17:20* [Comment . Like]

Tim Gleeve Can't say I'm *that* jealous. Exactly how many assignments are you trying to complete before flying out on Thursday? *Posted Tuesday 6th September at 17:20* [Comment . Like]

Kathy Bloomingdale Five. *Posted Tuesday 6th September at 17:21* [Comment . Like]

Madeline Cain Well that's a fire-brand to the backside if ever I saw one. *Posted Tuesday 6th September at 17:21* [Comment . Like]

Madeline Cain likes the page **If You Can't Handle Me Randomly Blurting Out Song Lyrics That Relate To What You Just Said, We Can't Be Friends.** [Like]

Tim Gleeve No matter how old or badass you are, when a two year old hands you a toy phone, you answer it. *Posted Tuesday 6th September at 17:40* [Comment . Like]

> **Madeline Cain** You're neither old, nor badass, Tim. You're kind of wiry. With love handles. *Posted Tuesday 6th September at 17:44* [Comment . Like]
>
> **Tim Gleeve** I'm sorry, Maddie, I don't have time to go through the finer points of badass-ery with you, I'm on the phone to Santa. *Posted Tuesday 6th September at 17:46* [Comment . Like]

Tim Gleeve poked you [Poke . Ignore]

Tim Gleeve threw a cow at your car [Throw a Bovine! . Ignore]

> **Confirmation** You wish to throw a camel instead? [Yes . I Have Changed My Mind]
>
> **Confirmation** Your camel has been thrown at Tim [ok]

Pet Society Request

Mike Cain has invited you to Pet Society where you can keep you Facebook friends as Pets! You can groom them, take them for walks, and if you have enough 'money' you can buy them away from a frien-emy. Groom your friends today! [Accept . Ignore]

Mike Cain I shall have three children: My first daughter will be called Stacy, so my wife will be Stacy's Mum, and yes, obviously she will have it 'going on'. My first son will be called Luke, so I can say 'Luke, I am your Father.' And my last son will be called Sparta, and whenever I serve him dinner I will cry, "For Sparta!" *Posted Tuesday 6th September at 18:10* [Comment . Like]

> **Madeline Cain** I'm not sure if you and Dad have had 'The Talk' yet, but for your information, having children requires a girl to *like* you. *Posted Tuesday 6th September at 18:15* [Comment . Like]

> **Mike Cain** I'm not sure if you and Dad have had 'The Talk' yet, but calling your children anything other than the above makes you a bore. *Posted Tuesday 6th September at 18:20* [Comment . Like]

Madeline Cain I love my dad! His story at dinner tonight: "They quoted me $1500 for the car service today. I told them, that's ok, because at least the car can fly now, right?" *Posted Tuesday 6th September at 19:37* [Comment . Like]

> **Tim Gleeve** I would have also attempted to secure a super hero cape in that bargain. *Posted Tuesday 6th September at 19:48* [Comment . Like]

Let Us Farewell Kathy... In Spirit... Because She's Too Much Of A Nerd For A Farewell Party.

EVENT INVITATION> Suggest your friends [Edit Event]

You are <u>Attending</u>. Public event

Time:	8 September at 10:35
Location:	Adelaide Airport
Created by:	Madeline Cain
More Info:	

> Seeing as Kathy was too busy nerding it out on the weekend (and mid-year, and the entirety of third term) to throw an actual going away party, I've decided to throw her a virtual one. Because even a digital party is preferable to no party at all.
>
> So bring your pixelated bowls of chips, videos of fireworks and appropriate BonVoyage memes and let's crash the servers!
>
> (Just, ah, no one invite Kathy's Mum, not only is she a buzzkill but I think she's still reeling that Kathy managed to pull this off.)
>
> Also, anyone who wants to take part in pretending Kathy is famous by crowding around her at the airport to say goodbye, please join us at the above time! Paparazzi cameras and headshots for autographing are the suggested optional props.

Write something...   [Share]

9

Kathy Bloomingdale Don't give me that guilt-trip! I'm only gone for six weeks, it's not like I'm dropping off the face of the planet. Being a hermit was my only option if I wanted to do this cultural exchange. If I had my way I would have done this years ago. But Mum's not a fish you can reel in on a line, she's a stone I've had to weather down over several years with the constant flow of my river. *Posted Tuesday 6th September at 20:17* [Comment . Like]

> **Tim Gleeve** That sounds so wrong. *Posted Tuesday 6th September at 20:21* [Comment . Like]

> **Kathy Bloomingdale** *Rolls eyes* It took me two years to even get her to a 'maybe' for this exchange and by then year twelve was looming. I think the only reason she said yes was because she was convinced I wouldn't be able to prepare and pass the STAT test in eight months to get my ATAR score. I fear this victory may affect my future bargaining power. *Posted Tuesday 6th September at 20:24* [Comment . Like]

> **Tim Gleeve** I find it interesting your own mother doesn't realise how stubborn you are. *Posted Tuesday 6th September at 20:24* [Comment . Like]

> **Madeline Cain** Mrs Bloomingdale lives in deep denial. I've been trying to calm her by claiming that at least this way, you'll get the whole wanting to be a costume designer thing out of your system. She seems to be under the misconception that this is a six week art class, rather than a world renowned short course for future designers. I'm sure that information just slipped your mind... *Posted Tuesday 6th September at 20:28* [Comment . Like]

> **Kathy Bloomingdale** Aw Mad! She doesn't understand it's not about the sparkles and red-carpet for me. That's the whole point of me doing this, to show her it's serious work, that I'm serious. Now I'll have to plough my way through all the now-that-you've-gotten-that-silly-fantasy-out-of-your-system   lectures

when I get home. *Posted Tuesday 6th September at 20:31* [Comment . Like]

Tim Gleeve Congrats on getting into Psych at Uni by the way. Now you can learn how to brainwash people. *Posted Tuesday 6th September at 20:31* [Comment . Like]

Madeline Cain I think she's off to a good start with her Mum ? She's got the reward/bribery dynamic down. *Posted Tuesday 6th September at 20:32* [Comment . Like]

Kathy Bloomingdale Ugh, Psych. It was the only way to get Mum off my back and convince her to sign my exchange permission slip. *Posted Tuesday 6th September at 20:33* [Comment . Like]

Tim Gleeve Being an 'exchange' does this mean we get someone to replace you? Are we going to get an Irish Kathy? One who says 'Top of the morning to ye' and organises potato eating competitions? *Posted Tuesday 6th September at 20:34* [Comment . Like]

Kathy Bloomingdale The word 'exchange' does indicate a trade of some type. While I can't guarantee what form this replacement will take, one thing I can assure you is the number of potato eating competitions they organise will be equivalent to the number of boomerang lessons I organise. AKA, zero. *Posted Tuesday 6th September at 20:36* [Comment . Like]

Mike Cain Now the school is mine! Moooo-ha-ha-ha-ha! *Posted Tuesday 6th September at 20:50* [Comment . Like]

Madeline Cain The only thing you've guaranteed by posting is that Kathy will return with a homemade straight jacket just for you. *Posted Tuesday 6th September at 20:52* [Comment . Like]

Kathy Bloomingdale Do you prefer white or crème Michael? *Posted Tuesday 6th September at 20:53* [Comment . Like]

Wyate Yosime I made you a virtual goodbye cake! Seeing as it doesn't have to follow the laws of nature it is three stories high and made of purple sunflowers. *Posted Tuesday 6th September at 20:17* [Comment . Like]

Diana Lynal Oh Kathy you're leaving?? What about graduation? I've barely seen you all semester! (I've been a bit wrapped up in Sam, sorry about that, lol!) We *have* to catch up before you go. *Posted Tuesday 6th September at 21:03* [Comment . Like]

> **Tim Gleeve** Get in line acquaintance! I don't think I can even remember what her face looks like, and we're supposed to be besties. *Posted Tuesday 6th September at 21:13* [Comment . Like]

> **Madeline Cain** I can't believe a teenage boy used the word 'besties'. She'll be back for term four, Diana. This is if she doesn't find a pot of gold at the end of a rainbow and abandon us for a life rich mansions and holidays in Tahiti. *Posted Tuesday 6th September at 21:31* [Comment . Like]

Kathy Bloomingdale JUST handed in the last assignment! Now for a round of Speed Packing! *Posted Wednesday 7th September at 14:50* [Comment . Like]

Tim Gleeve Birthday ninjas. They sneak up on you like regular ninjas, only instead of nun-chucks they're armed with cake. *Posted Wednesday 7th September at 16:30* [Comment . Like]

> **Madeline Cain** Kinda like a clown but in black? *Posted Wednesday 7th September at 17:00* [Comment . Like]

> **Tim Gleeve** *Birthday Ninja Target acquired.* *November 7th

Locked in.* *Posted Wednesday 7th September at 17:15* [Comment . Like]

Lulu Tanaki Christening invitations sent! I have the biggest collection of paper cuts as a result. Less Edward-Scissor-hands, more scissored-hands. *Posted Wednesday 7th September at 18:12* [Comment . Like]

> **Madeline Cain** I swear, a paper cut is mother earth's way of saying, "You cut me down, I cut you up." *Posted Wednesday 7th September at 18:24* [Comment . Like]

Madeline Cain A conversation between my dad and my brother:

Dad: You know what sucks?

Mike: A vacuum.

Dad: Well yes, but do you know what sucks in a metaphorical sense?

Mike: Black holes?

Dad: Okay, let's go a different route. You know what's not cool?

Mike: Lava?

Dad: I disown you as my son.

Should have happened years ago in my opinion. *Posted Wednesday 7th September at 19:41* [Comment . Like]

> **Tim Gleeve** Are you sure they're not rehearsing a comedy sketch of puns? Or it could prove your father's a robot and unable to continue a conversation until the correct answer has been given. *Posted Wednesday 7th September at 19:52* [Comment . Like]

> **Mike Cain** "No, what?" is not an answer this genius is willing to give. If you phrase it like a question, I'm gonna give you an

answer. *Posted Wednesday 7th September at 19:56* [Comment . Like]

Madeline Cain If you're a genius, I live in a castle made of fairy floss. *Posted Wednesday 7th September at 19:58* [Comment . Like]

Kate Nikle likes the page **Read It Like It's Being Screamed By Animal From The Muppets.** [Like]

Mike Cain The left wing said they'd abolish poverty, the right wing said they'd abolish bureaucracy. Odin said he'd abolish ice giants. Where are the ice giants? Vote Odin! *Mic drop* *High fives all round* *Breakfast Club freeze frame* *Roll credits.* *Posted Wednesday 7th September at 21:41* [Comment . Like]

> **Madeline Cain** Can anyone else see Mike changing his name by deed poll and registering the Asguard party in future ploys to take over the world? *Posted Wednesday 7th September at 21:47* [Comment . Like]
>
> **Tim Gleeve** I do! I can also see him running through parliament house in a loin cloth knocking out senators with a hammer. *Posted Wednesday 7th September at 21:48* [Comment . Like]

Isabelle Haigh A few weeks ago I got another kitten. His name is MacGyver, and he only has three legs. The RSPCA don't know how he lost his leg, but I assume it was a shark attack, like that surfing girl in Hawaii. *Posted Wednesday 7th September at 22:30* [Comment . Like]

Tim Gleeve Hello Rioters. Look at your friend, now back to me, now to your friend, now back to me. Sadly, he isn't me; but if he stopped his antisocial behaviour and started handing out CVs he could be like me. Look down, now back up. Where are we? We're at an interview with the man your friend could work for! What's in his hand? That CV he wrote so he could get a haircut and get a real job. Look again, that paper is now money! Anything is possible when you get a job and stop looting. I'm at a desk. *Posted Thursday 8th September at 16:16* [Comment . Like]

> **Virginia Lowe** Timothy, that's a very narrow minded view of the whole London riot situation. They've been discriminated against in a classist society! If it was as easy as 'getting a job' don't you think they'd do that rather than running terrified through the streets, or having to steal food to survive? *Posted Thursday 8th September at 16:30* [Comment . Like]

> **Tim Gleeve** *Snort* Poor naive little Vee. I think they'd rather score some free shit and re-enact an action scene from a Hollywood blockbuster complete with chairs and shattered glass than put on a tie, wear Old Spice and be responsible. What they need is a water cannon to the face and their bum super glued to a chair. *Posted Thursday 8th September at 16:35* [Comment . Like]

> **Virginia Lowe** The next thing you'll be suggesting is sending them off to Australia in boats! *Posted Thursday 8th September at 16:37* [Comment . Like]

> **Tim Gleeve** All I'm saying is, when I become President of the World I will give them the choice between a job and walking naked in Christmas Island covered in crab bait. *Posted Thursday 8th September at 16:40* [Comment . Like]

> **Virginia Lowe** You're impossible! And insensitive! And... And.... *Posted Thursday 8th September at 16:40* [Comment . Like]

> **Madeline Cain** A jerk? *Posted Thursday 8th September at 16:41* [Comment . Like]

> **Virginia Lowe** 100%. *Posted Thursday 8th September at 16:41* [Comment . Like]

Tim Gleeve Gee, thanks for your support, Maddie. *Posted Thursday 8th September at 16:42* [Comment . Like]

Madeline Cain Anything I can do to help, Mr President. *Posted Thursday 8th September at 16:43* [Comment . Like]

Kathy Bloomingdale Flight to Heathrow was virtually empty. I had a strong desire to steal all the extra pillows and blankets and make a fort. *Posted Friday 9th September at 07:10* [Comment . Like]

Have You Crash Landed? Or Are You In Leprechaun Land? [New Message]

[Back to messages. Mark as unread . Report spam . Delete]

Between **Tim Gleeve**, **Kathy Bloomingdale** and **You**.

———————

Madeline Cain 9 September 2011 at 20:00

You've been MIA a *really* long time, Kathy. I know you said it would take something stupid like 24 hours to get there, but it's been a dozen hours over that. Have you been kidnapped by Leprechauns? Or fallen into some European equivalent of the Bermuda Triangle?

Tim Gleeve 9 September 2011 at 20:10 [Report]

Or did they fill you up with so much Guinness on arrival that you still can't type straight?

Madeline Cain 9 September 2011 at 20:12

Guinness? She's still a month off eighteen!

Tim Gleeve 9 September 2011 at 20:14 [Report]

I hear in Ireland that as long as your chin is higher than the bar, you're old enough to drink. At least *someone* should be having fun in year twelve.

Madeline Cain 9 September 2011 at 20:16

Well it's certainly not me! Every time I turn a corner at school there is yet *another* teacher asking me which university course I've decided on. I'm not sure what epiphany they think I've come across in the 45mins since they last asked me. Either they're all gold-fish at heart, or they're expecting angel intervention at any moment.

Tim Gleeve 9 September 2011 at 20:17 [Report]

I read that as Angle Intervention and immediately went to Transformer land. I don't know what you're complaining about, clearly after twelve years of school you should know what you want to do *forever* :p

Madeline Cain 9 September 2011 at 20:20

On a scale of zero to completely unhelpful you are a ten.

I don't know how they expect me to decide the rest of my life at seventeen (clearly you just rolled dice for your career path). I'm good a lots of stuff, but just because you're good at something doesn't mean you want to marry it, or even like the damn thing. Take maths for example. Sure, me and quadratic equations get on, but it doesn't mean I'm going to move into their house and start eating their Pi.

Did you see what I did there?

Tim Gleeve 9 September 2011 at 20:21 [Report]

Groan Are you sure you're not heading for a career as a mathematician? Only they make those lame-ass jokes.

Madeline Cain 9 September 2011 at 20:24

Said the guy who knows Pi to 100 decimal places. Because that will soooooo come in handy in an IT career. How is it someone so specially gifted at pissing people off has a traineeship lined up? Can you see into the future? Do you have some sort of Harry Potter time turner you're hording? Because I'll fight you for it (and win!). If not, then how is it you and Kathy already have your dreams lined up and I'm the only target left for overenthusiastic educators?

Kathy Bloomingdale 9 September 2011 at 20:26 [Report]

If I could see into the future I wouldn't have gotten on that God damn plane. I almost died for my dream. DIED.

Madeline Cain 9 September 2011 at 20:26

WHAT?!

Tim Gleeve 9 September 2011 at 20:26 [Report]

Dude, we were just joking about the Bermuda Triangle thing. No need to play up a little turbulence.

Kathy Bloomingdale 9 September 2011 at 20:29 [Report]

Turbulence!? This was not turbulence! You passing gas is turbulence. This was winds from the four corners of the earth having a rave party around *my* aeroplane. There was luggage falling out of overhead lockers, and oxygen masks dropping from the ceiling. Admittedly the masks coming down was a malfunction, but the plane was literally trying to shake itself apart!

Madeline Cain 9 September 2011 at 20:31

Eep! I'm so sorry I made that plane crash joke in the subject heading. Are you ok? Which flight was this? You seemed fine in that post you made at Heathrow (BTW you should have totally made a blanket *mansion*).

Tim Gleeve 9 September 2011 at 20:32 [Report]

The turbulence was for how long exactly? Because it sounds like the oxygen masks made you panic more than was warranted.

Kathy Bloomingdale 9 September 2011 at 20:35 [Report]

Oh, because the first thing everyone does when their plane is trying to disassemble around them is *time how long it jerks!* Sod off Tim, watches are for rational life moments.

It was the Heathrow to Dublin flight. A smaller plane with wings *way* too flexible. Other than developing a life-long plane phobia, I'm fine. I didn't message because the college were settling us into our rooms and then gave us an introduction to the campus and course.

Tim Gleeve 9 September 2011 at 20:36 [Report]

Well, that's unfortunate, you have to fly home in October. I'd get your Mum to mail some sleeping pills ASAP. The flight attendants will need them to get you on that plane. That or the straight jacket you're putting together for Mike.

Kathy Bloomingdale 9 September 2011 at 20:37 [Report]

Don't you dare tell my mother! She'll have a fit and I'll never, ever be allowed to leave my house again. Ugh! I'm getting worked up just thinking about it. Let's talk about something else. Anything else.

Madeline Cain 9 September 2011 at 20:38

Like how the bloody hell is Ireland?!

Tim Gleeve 9 September 2011 at 20:38 [Report]

Like how Maddie's having her mid-life crisis at seventeen?

Kathy Bloomingdale 9 September 2011 at 20:42 [Report]

Wet and green. You know that book '48 Shades of Brown' they forced us to read last year in English? Well there are about double the shades of green here, it barely felt like a city as we splashed through on the bus. It hasn't stopped raining since we arrived (not a good omen for the return plane ride…) so exploring has been restricted to the indoor variety and what we could see out the bus window. The buildings are all so *old,* and there are cobble-stone streets, *actual cobble-stone streets!* It seems like there's a pub on every corner. And the accents, Maddie!

You wouldn't believe how sensual it sounds to the ears; all soft vowels, hard consonants and dropped Gs. I sometimes completely missed what people were saying because I was just listening to that sweet sound buffet.

Madeline Cain 9 September 2011 at 20:42

Mmm, Irish accents. That's almost worth a dodgy plane flight. What else?

Kathy Bloomingdale 9 September 2011 at 20:46 [Report]

It's hilly, the buildings are greyish with alleyways tagged with hundreds of spray-painted letters. Oh! And there's a massive river running through the middle (and it's not a dammed creek pretending to be a river like the Torrens in Adelaide!). That's about the sum of it so far.

But what's this about Maddie having a mid-life crisis? Do you *still* not know what it is you want to do with yourself after school, Mad? I kinda blocked most of the outside world out for the last six months. Sorry, I'm such a bad friend ?

Tim Gleeve 9 September 2011 at 20:48 [Report]

I haven't seen anyone this indecisive since Marley Greenwood couldn't decide which way to go around a tree and ended up riding her bike straight into it. In fact, Maddie's been so indecisive she's let Miss Kennedy gang press her into attending an Early Admissions interview at the University of Adelaide.

Madeline Cain 9 September 2011 at 20:49

I wasn't gang pressed! Miss Kennedy was just really persuasive when it comes to chemistry degrees.

Tim Gleeve 9 September 2011 at 20:49 [Report]

Yeah, scary persuasive, as in lean-on-you-until-you-submit-to-her-will-or-explode-like-potassium-in-water persuasive.

Madeline Cain 9 September 2011 at 20:49

At least she didn't jump out from behind a shrubbery like Mr Pennisi.

Tim Gleeve 9 September 2011 at 20:50 [Report]

Or pack your school bag full of Architecture books like Ms Lambert.

Kathy Bloomingdale 9 September 2011 at 20:50 [Report]

Geez, is there a betting pool in the teachers' lounge or something? What's an Early Admissions Interview?

Tim Gleeve 9 September 2011 at 20:52 [Report]

It's where they interview crazy people who want to start uni two months early. Apparently you finish the degree earlier but you only graduate as a puddle because the stress has caused you to melt.

Kathy Bloomingdale 9 September 2011 at 20:53 [Report]

Right, you've just described my last, never-to-be-repeated, six months. So you want to be a chemist, Maddie?

Madeline Cain 9 September 2011 at 20:54

No. Yes. Maybe? I mean Kennedy's passionate about it, and like she says I've aced chemistry so far. Maybe I can be that passionate once I, you know, do lots of it.

Tim Gleeve 9 September 2011 at 20:55 [Report]

Yeah but you've aced everything so far: Graphics, History, English, Maths. It's sickening really how much talent rests in that little head of yours.

Kathy Bloomindale 9 September 2011 at 20:57 [Report]

You're going for an Early Admissions interview and you're not even sure you want to be a chemist?? It might seem free but you do know you have to pay the government back the money you borrow to pay for your degree, right? Each course for a science degree costs like, $2000. You have to do four a semester and have two semesters for four years.

Madeline Cain 9 September 2011 at 21:02

They cost what?! That is an ass-butt amount to pay! I don't want to do that!

Ugh, I hate this to and fro, I feel like someone's dressed me in a tutu and spun me around until I puke. That's the problem with being good at the 'smart people' subjects, Tim. The moment you suggest something other than going straight to uni, or doing a course other than the hardest subject you take at school, people stare at you like you've got ten heads and a monster growing out of each armpit. *But you're so smart? Why would you want to waste all you've achieved? Why don't you want to be like me?*

I disappoint everyone. That's why I said yes to her. It's not like any of my other courses offer more exciting prospects.

Kathy Bloomingdale 9 September 2011 at 21:03 [Report]

What about art? You like art.

Madeline Cain 9 September 2011 at 21:05

Yes I *like* it, but I'm not actually any good. My drawings are so bad I'm surprised my stick people don't revolt and set themselves on fire. I like it because I don't have to be good, I don't have to prove anything, it is a release. I think people would pay me to just stop hurting their eyes.

Tim Gleeve 9 September 2011 at 21:06 [Report]

I can attest to that. There was this one painting which was a blob on another blob with some leg like blobs and I thought it was a snowman eating a person. Turns out it was meant to be a Picasso imitation.

Madeline Cain 9 September 2011 at 21:08

I got a C for that piece. That was probably warranted. It was heaps fun to do though, I was finding paint in all sorts of crevasses over the next week. I think the only thing I got an A in was the photography module we did. Mrs Cook is the only person who hasn't tried to give me a surprise heart-attack via shrubbery. That's why I keep doing art.

Kathy Bloomingdale 9 September 2011 at 21:09 [Report]

What do you actually *want* then? Out of a job I mean?

Madeline Cain 9 September 2011 at 21:12

Shrug. To not be bored? I've always imagined I'd have grand adventures, but the careers being forced on me don't seem to lead that way, not like yours have. I'm so jealous of you guys. Knowing what you want to do in life.

Tim Gleeve 9 September 2011 at 21:13 [Report]

Internet is life Maddie, I don't know why you'd consider anything else for a career.

Madeline Cain 9 September 2011 at 21:14

Bet you've carefully calculated the minimum amount of work you need to do to pass year twelve too.

Tim Gleeve 9 September 2011 at 21:14 [Report]

That's true. No use stressing when you can coast through life.

Madeline Cain 9 September 2011 at 21:15

Bah humbug! May the internet bring you nothing but Lol Catz!

Kathy Bloomingdale 9 September 2011 at 21:17 [Report]

I stumbled across designing only by luck. My Mum picked up a book on costume design at a charity sale thinking it was a picture book. There's always a moment in life that flips that passion on like a light switch. Yours is still coming, that's all. I have to do crap I don't want to do too, like a year of Psych at uni so I can build up an application to get into NIDA (not that Mum knows *whistles guiltily*). How about that careers test we did? What careers did yours suggest?

Madeline Cain 9 September 2011 at 21:23

You mean the Random-Job-Generator? Because that's what it felt like, it just threw careers at me to see if one stuck like a piece of cooked spaghetti. I did not one, but *three* careers tests, because the guidance councillor thought the first two tests weren't accurate enough for my 'complex tastes'. It turns out my subconscious is just as indecisive as my conscious.

How can you get any sense out of a program that asks you to decide your top choice between: 'Liaising with wholesale companies about new swimwear socks', 'Patrolling in a boat looking for holes in fishing nets' and 'Monitoring absenteeism and work output for factory employees'? One gave me a choice between becoming a senator or a scientist (because that's totally the two main job groups). Please excuse me while I gouge my eyes out.

Tim Gleeve 9 September 2011 at 21:25 [Report]

Then there was that test in which you answered 'slightly interested' to all 52 questions except the one that asked if you were interested in investigating crimes, to which you put 'interested'.

Madeline Cain 9 September 2011 at 21:27

Come on! Answering anything other than 'interested' on that question makes you look like a dickhead. Or a potential serial killer. It was a trick question that ended up with me getting a recommendation to become a public service employee. Seriously. As if anyone actually sets out to work in government voluntarily. Apparently I would 'excel' in service occupations. This list included 'Personal Assistant', 'Advertising', 'Librarian' and 'Hotel/Motel Manager'.

Tim Gleeve 9 September 2011 at 21:28 [Report]

Sexy librarian?

Madeline Cain 9 September 2011 at 21:28

So sexy. You'd never be able to touch this.

Kathy Bloomingdale 9 September 2011 at 21:29 [Report]

I feel I'm the only one remembering your short-lived career at McDonalds where you over-salted the fries of people who were rude to you. I don't want to think of the depths of your revenge if you ran a hotel.

Tim Gleeve 9 September 2011 at 21:30 [Report]

I feel it would involve plain clothed hotel employees pretending to be guests just so they could spill various food and drink items on designer clothing.

Kathy Bloomingdale 9 September 2011 at 21:32 [Report]

That's why we don't let you near people, Tim; you in the service industry would be diabolical. All those careers sound consistent, Mad. What confused the councillor into giving you two more tests?

Madeline Cain 9 September 2011 at 21:33

Oh, they weren't all together, they were interspersed with such career suggestions as: animal trainer, florist, archaeologist, art therapist, food & wine scientist, cheese sculptor, wax figure maker, embalmer, and sports consultant.

Tim Gleeve 9 September 2011 at 21:35 [Report]

The sporting world must be in dire need if they're looking for someone like you. Being coached by you would go something like this: "Now go out there and don't fall over!"

Kathy Bloomingdale 9 September 2011 at 21:36 [Report]

Embalmer? As in making dead people look like they're just sleeping at their own funeral??

Madeline Cain 9 September 2011 at 21:38

Oh no, that's a different job again. An embalmer stops the bodies from decomposing for long enough to bury them. But wait until you hear the number one career recommendation. I'm pretty sure I need a sex change for this one.

Tim Gleeve 9 September 2011 at 21:40 [Report]

Oooh ooh! Do they want you to be a drag queen? No wait! A male stripper? A body builder?

Madeline Cain 9 September 2011 at 21:40

No, no and no. The honour of top career option goes to, 'Minister/ Priest/Rabbi'.

Kathy Bloomingdale 9 September 2011 at 21:43 [Report]

Wow. Were you asked to choose between salvation and eternal damnation at some point? How can the test ask you to choose between marketing swimwear socks and looking for holes in nets and completely miss the question of, 'do you have man bits or lady bits?'

Tim Gleeve 9 September 2011 at 21:45 [Report]

I don't know… With a sex change, a religious change and some identity fraud for the third option, I think Maddie's got herself a winning career tending to the Jewish flock. Maybe she can part the Torrens River and lead them to a land of better internet.

Kathy Bloomingdale 9 September 2011 at 21:46 [Report]

Now I understand why you've clung to Mrs Kennedy like a drop bear.

Madeline Cain 9 September 2011 at 21:48

I'm not *clinging* to anything. I'm going with the least stupid (though no less terrifying) option. At the moment that happens to be an Early Admissions interview tomorrow. Which, like everything else that happens while you're away, I will tell you about via Facebook notes. That way Tim doesn't keep interrupting me with every stray fart that passes through his head.

Tim Gleeve 9 September 2011 at 21:49 [Report]

Pot calling the kettle black there.

Kathy Bloomingdale 9 September 2011 at 21:50 [Report]

Yes please! I expect everything chronicled in incredibly fine detail so I don't feel so homesick. And no letting my replacement brainwash you into liking them better, ok?!

Tim Gleeve 9 September 2011 at 21:52 [Report]

No need to worry on that front. Your replacement is a very odd egg. I mean super odd. As in she stood out the front of school today wearing a t-shirt that said 'Life' on it and as everyone was leaving she handed them lemons. Actual lemons.

Kathy Bloomingdale 9 September 2011 at 21:52 [Report]

That's very… meta. Did anyone make lemonade?

Tim Gleeve 9 September 2011 at 21:52 [Report]

I'm pretty sure the majority of people turned them into projectile weapons.

Madeline Cain 9 September 2011 at 21:54

'When life hands you lemons, squish them in the eyes of your enemy', seems to be the motto of Marrayatville High students. You're replacement's name is Claire Holderness. She's at least a head shorter than you, black hair cut in a pixie bob, bright blue eyes and has the most musical accent (you were on the money with that one). It was her first day today and she mustn't have been told about the uniform policy because she was dressed all in black, except of course for the large, white 'Life' across her chest.

Tim Gleeve 9 September 2011 at 21:55 [Report]

Kim Trist asked her whose funeral it was. She just looked from Kim, to Krystal, to Kylie and said, "I haven't decided yet."

Kathy Bloomingdale 9 September 2011 at 21:55 [Report]

Snort! She's not out to make friends, is she?

Tim Gleeve 9 September 2011 at 21:56 [Report]

Frankly, I don't think she gives a crap. Unlike, Maddie.

Madeline Cain 9 September 2011 at 21:58

Fine, do you want me to admit it? I was railroaded by a teacher into a potentially horrible mistake. I care what people think. I want people to be proud of me. Is that so wrong? But I won't know if it's a mistake or not until I check it out, will I? Then I'll ask Kathy's advice, because yours is about as helpful as a cat in a cookie jar. At least I'm not handing acidic projectiles to twelve year olds like Irish Kathy. I mean Claire.

Tim Gleeve 9 September 2011 at 21:59 [Report]

I forgive you your sins, Father Cain.

Madeline Cain 9 September 2011 at 21:59

Just for that I'm going to have all my panic attacks around you. Potentially on you. By the time I settle on a career path you're going to feel positively schizophrenic.

Kathy Bloomingdale 9 September 2011 at 22:02 [Report]

Ok, I can see this spiralling into the depths of that name-calling MSN chat from 2008. So I'm tapping out before the poo-flinging begins. Maddie, make sure you keep me up-to-date on all the goss while I'm gone. Including lemon girl. Don't be nervous about the interview tomorrow, if it doesn't feel right for you then go with your gut. Goodbye lovely people!

Madeline Cain 9 September 2011 at 22:03

BYE! I'll try to keep this one in line while you're gone.

Tim Gleeve 9 September 2011 at 22:03 [Report]

So no to Rabbi Cain?

Tim Gleeve 9 September 2011 at 22:03 [Report]

How about Father Mad?

Tim Gleeve 9 September 2011 at 22:04 [Report]

No, definitely Mad Pastor Cain. Makes it sound like a disease you contract from spaghetti.

Kathy Bloomingdale Advice is just advice. It's not an equation. It's not the instruction manual for Ikea furniture (which are admittedly super-bloody-vague anyway). You're your own Muse… *Head desk* who am I kidding? I should have listened to Mum. *Posted Friday 9th September at 20:32* [Comment . Like]

> **Madeline Cain** This sounds ominous. Which of your mother's ten commandments did you break? *Posted Friday 9th September at 20:40* [Comment . Like]
>
> **Tim Gleeve** I don't want to live in a world where Mrs Bloomingdale is right about anything. Say it isn't so! *Posted Friday 9th September at 20:45* [Comment . Like]
>
> **Kathy Bloomingdale** You remember how I refused to learn sewing because my Mother said, 'all proper young ladies know how to sew'? *Posted Friday 9th September at 20:48* [Comment . Like]
>
> **Madeline Cain** I have vague recollections. *Posted Friday 9th September at 20:49* [Comment . Like]
>
> **Tim Gleeve** It's like the 1950's in your house, I'm not surprised. *Posted Friday 9th September at 20:50* [Comment . Like]
>
> **Kathy Bloomingdale** Yeah, well, it turns out all good designers need to know how to sew. And every single person here knows how. Except me. I'm undone by my own mother-daughter rebellion, and it's only the first week! This is all much harder than I thought it would be… *Posted Friday 9th September at 20:52* [Comment . Like]
>
> **Tim Gleeve** Is convincing yourself you were justified in ignoring your Mother's advice working out for you? Built any

Ikea furniture out of regret yet? *Posted Friday 9th September at 20:53* [Comment . Like]

Kathy Bloomingdale No furniture, but if Ikea provides DIY weapons you'll be the first to know. *Posted Friday 9th September at 20:53* [Comment . Like]

Madeline Cain Says the man who failed abysmally at putting together his Ikea desk chair. Don't freak out Kathy, you can learn this. Just think, you already know how to draw a killer design, now you just have to learn the extra bits and bobs. It's why you're there. Forget what other people do and don't know. *Posted Friday 9th September at 20:55* [Comment . Like]

Kathy Bloomingdale Well, the girl next to me did look like she was building a tuxedo for a whale... *Posted Friday 9th September at 20:56* [Comment . Like]

Madeline Cain That's the spirit! Go forth and make Mike's straight jacket, I'm counting on you. And a gag for Tim while you're at it. *Posted Friday 9th September at 20:57* [Comment . Like]

Derek Chan Almost ran over a bat tonight. What kind of bad luck does THAT bring? *Posted Friday 9th September at 21:24* [Comment . Like]

Tim Gleeve It makes your flying car crash. *Posted Friday 9th September at 21:26* [Comment . Like]

Kathy Bloomingdale Being mauled by an angry vampire I suspect. *Posted Friday 9th September at 21:27* [Comment . Like]

Madeline Cain Bat luck. Obviously. *Posted Friday 9th September at 21:30* [Comment . Like]

Kathy Bloomingdale I just cut my finger open. On my toothbrush.

Yes. Shut up. I'm talented, okay? *Posted Friday 9th September at 23:03* [Comment . Like]

> **Tim Gleeve** Only in Ireland. *Posted Friday 9th September at 23:10* [Comment . Like]

Kyle Traybna Wow, what a stunningly beautiful day! These are the kinds of days that make me feel truly alive! *Posted Saturday 10th September at 07:03* [Comment . Like]

Kate Nikle likes the page **"I Have Read And Agree To The Terms And Conditions" – Biggest. Lie. Ever.** [Like]

Madeline Cain Tim Gleeve Why do you always wear clothes that makes you look like a 1950's life guard to the beach? *Posted Saturday 10th September at 09:45* [Comment . Like]

> **Mike Cain** Or the bastard son of Ronald McDonald. *Posted Saturday 10th September at 10:00* [Comment . Like]

> **Tim Gleeve** If you want to turn a vibrant shade of tomato, you go right ahead. I'm a firm believer in NOT looking like a Redskin. *Posted Saturday 10th September at 10:10* [Comment . Like]

Madeline Cain Everything happens for a reason. Sometimes, the reason is you're stupid and make bad decisions. Only time will tell for me. *Posted Saturday 10th September at 13:19* [Comment . Like]

> **Mike Cain** Good to see you're owning up to your mutant superpowers. While the powers of stupidity and bad decision making aren't as cool as shooting a web from your butt, the results are at least as entertaining. *Posted Saturday 10th September at 13:29* [Comment . Like]

> **Madeline Cain** At least I aspire to do more than fart the

alphabet. *Posted Saturday 10th September at 13:34* [Comment . Like]

Tim Gleeve Aspire to do more of what? *Posted Saturday 10th September at 13:38* [Comment . Like]

Madeline Cain Your guess is as good as mine. I'm just hoping today's decision doesn't come back to bite me in the arse. *Posted Saturday 10th September at 13:42* [Comment . Like]

Tim Gleeve Shall I attempt to divine the future from pelican entrails for you? *Posted Saturday 10th September at 13:48* [Comment . Like]

Madeline Cain That's sweet, but on the grounds of animal rights I'm gonna have to decline. *Posted Saturday 10th September at 13:57* [Comment . Like]

Do You Have An Appointment? Or, 365 Days Of Fun

NOTES > My Notes [Write a note]

By **Madeline Cain.** Saturday, 10 September 2011 at 16:50.

I'm gonna put it out there, I failed something on purpose. That purpose may have seen me not listen particularly closely to questions being asked. That purpose may have resulted in me looking the admissions board in the eye and confirming that growing ears on the backs of human test subjects *was* a good idea. That purpose may have been to prevent the epic freak out and melt down of a young Australian woman who hasn't quite managed to pick her tree from the forest yet. And that something... *may* have been an interview.

Yes, I know it's not like me, failing things on purpose is surely a Madeline paradox, but the choose-your-future-time-bomb was about to go off and it was either re-wire, or explode.

In the end it was all part of a carefully thought out plan... a plan I created on the elevator ride to the interview room. While chatting to Irish Kathy behind a desk. I understand this doesn't make much sense at the moment, but it will once I explain.

It was a very weird elevator ride.

I was wearing my most professional clothes (a black skirt and white shirt I stole from Mum) as I approached the Napier building at Adelaide Uni. The visit was not off to an auspicious start. There are a lot of good looking buildings on campus, beautiful limestone halls, red brick lecture theatres and sandstone libraries. But the Napier building is one of the ugliest I've ever seen, all tinted windows and grey pebbled walls, I felt like I'd time warped to the 70's. The inside wasn't any prettier as I tried to ignore the dozens of tattered academic posters lining the hospital-like walls. If I was looking for omens, that was bad omen number one.

The second omen came when I was waiting for the Elevator of Patience. It must be hand-cranked by elves, that's how slow this hunk-of-junk was. It gave me more than enough time to work myself into a mess. *What in God's name are you doing? This isn't what you want. But you don't know what you DO want. So maybe you're just being ridiculous. But this isn't what life is, right? Just doing stuff you kind of like? It's possible to love your job, right? Or do you just pick the thing you suck at the least? Holy shit what if I'm in the same job for 50 years?? Am I over thinking this? Am I thinking at all? Let's see, seven times eight equals…shit! Equals what? A number? A wingding? A box of cats??*

These were just some of the thoughts fuelling the whirlwind that churned my guts into a tight ball of nausea. As you can see I had no idea what I was doing, and was digging myself an even deeper hole to break my legs in.

The third omen was heralded by the dull chime of the elevator which opened on a girl. A girl behind a wooden desk that almost stretched from wall to elevator wall.

"Do you have an appointment?" she asked, looking up from a large notebook.

Our eyes locked and recognition came simultaneously. Behind the desk sat Claire – aka, Irish Kathy. We were stunned into surprised silence for so long that the elevator chimed once again and the doors started to close. Quick as the Flash Claire whipped out a long pole and struck it against the closing door, forcing it open.

"I know you," she said.

"Yep."

She cocked head to the side, blue eyes boring into mine. Her hand rapped against the desk jerking me out of my hypnotic state. "Madeline! Your name is Madeline. I knew I knew it." She grinned as though she'd won a prize.

"And you're Claire. Why are you…" I gestured at the desk.

She let lose an infectious chuckle. "Just havin' a bit of crack. A lot of crack actually. You'll probably see for yourself in a minute. You?"

I froze, eyes wide. The elevator chimed three times, and I

automatically stepped in. With a potential drug addict. Oh my god. Claire didn't make any move to withdraw her stick, holding it firmly against the door with her head cocked, waiting for her answer.

I licked my lips. "I'm just, ah, doing this stupid interview thing. For early admission. To get into this, course, degree, thing, with the paper. And the jobs. It's gonna be great."

She lifted an eyebrow. "When you tell a lie like that you've got to back it with *some* enthusiasm."

I blinked. Holy crap, what had I just said? Did I somehow drop in a line about drugs without realising it?

"Hmmm," she said tapping her lips. "It's not just lack of enthusiasm, you're down right terrified. Look at you. You're shaking like a Beyonce backup dancer." She reclined in her chair as the elevator buzzed again. Then again. Then louder. Then longer.

"Ah, maybe we should–"

Claire held up a hand cutting me off. "Can I help you? Do you have an appointment?"

I frowned and opened my mouth to respond, when a voice behind me replied, "Pardon?"

"An appointment, an appointment good fellow. Do you have one? At all?" Rather than sounding ludicrous, Claire's smooth Irish lint gave the demands the sound of authority.

"Did you call ahead?" she pressed, "Make a time? Set a date? Receive an invitation paper or otherwise?"

"I... what?"

I turned to see a man in his mid–twenties, dressed in cotton, draw-string pants and long-sleeved Indian style shirt. He ran his hand through his hair exposing a receding hairline.

"I don't need an appointment, I take this elevator every day," he said, eyes nervously taking in the desk, the non–lit lamp, and the massive stick in Claire's hand.

Claire gave an exasperated sigh. "I should have expected this level of incompetence on day one. You're not the fizziest six-pack in the shop are you? Clearly the rules have changed. You need an appointment."

At a loss for words he reverted to stating the obvious. "But, you're in an elevator."

"Yes, it saves people using electricity on unnecessary elevator trips." Claire yawned, looking at her watch. "I don't know what to say other than the Home Guard have assigned me to this position to regulate access to the higher ups. If you want to make an appointment you're going to have to come back to me dressed in something that can pull off a bowtie."

The confusion on the man's face made him look like a droopy jowled dog as he mouthed the words *home guard* to himself, trying to pull some knowledge from the depths of his brain of a department I assume Claire created on the spot. Probably a code phrase to test if he wanted crack.

"You can try the stairs of course. The stair receptionist may be more lenient than myself," she said.

"There's a *stair* receptionist?" he asked.

"Naturally. Now if you'll excuse me I must finalise this young lady's appointment."

The man treated me to a bewildered look, then took one step, then two down the corridor before finally setting off for the distant stairwell at the end of the hall.

Claire gave a self-satisfied chuckle and picked up a glass of water resting on the desk. "Best crack ever. Now, where were we?" she asked taking a sip.

Unable to hold it in any longer I said, "Soooo. You're doing drugs. In an elevator. At a desk."

Water burst from Claire's mouth, covering me from head to foot. She choked, "What the hell are you talking about?"

I couldn't believe she was trying to shore up that crumbling façade. "The crack. You said you were having crack!"

She stared at me, water dripping down her chin, stick hovering in her hand. Her face crumpled, her shoulders shook and she let forth a big, gasping laugh. Her pale face was red in seconds, tears streaming from her eyes.

"You thought! Crack! Oh my... "

"I don't get it." I shook my head at her, wiping ineffectually at my shirt front now covered in transparent dots.

"Crack means *fun* you daft Aussie! I'm having a lot of fun! I thought you spoke English over here."

"Not your warped, Irish version," I snapped.

But I couldn't keep up the annoyed front for long. A manic giggle bubbled up and joined hers as we drowned out the now constant dinging of the elevator bell with our whoops.

"Gosh, was that why you were sweating so much? You thought you'd happened upon a drug dealer?" she asked, wiping her eyes. "Welcome to university kids! Here, have a line. Take a cookie. Shove a pill up the wazoo."

"Oh no I was like that before I knew you were in there," I assured her.

Claire pursed her lips. "Well that doesn't sound good. If you're freaking out so much why did you come? In fact, why are you freaking out?"

The elevator bell had almost become a siren by then, loud, consistent tolls drawing the attention of several passers-by.

"Look, mind if we let the doors close now? I don't want to get in trouble."

"You don't like ruffling feathers do you?"

"No, I don't," I said forcefully. "Now can we go?"

"You're avoiding the question."

I sighed. "One of my teachers put a lot of effort into setting this up for me. She's expecting me to do well."

"But…"

"It's all happening a little too fast. That's all."

Claire bounced her stick up and down, her face thoughtful. "Did you ask her to set it up?"

"Nooooo… She asked me what I thought, and I said it sounded okay and she just… did it."

"And you didn't want to ruffle any feathers."

"Yeah, something like that," I said, looking at my feet.

"Hmmm." Claire suddenly lifted her stick vertical, storing it behind her.

As though expecting interference at any moment the elevator door slammed shut and the box lumbered into motion. Blessed silence filled the space. I shifted uncomfortably under Claire's silent regard.

"So this interview is just for early admission right? If things don't go well it doesn't stop you from applying for a normal semester?" she asked.

"Yes, that's right. It's for people who are smart and… and want to do things faster I suppose."

"Doing things faster is over rated," she said lightly, looking down at her nails. "Sounds like people are rushing things for you. But it's your life. If you want to give yourself more time it's pretty simple."

"Yes?" The word burst from my lips.

She shrugged. "You should just screw up the interview. Who's gonna know?"

The elevator doors opened behind me as I tried to get my thoughts in order so I could explain exactly *why* it wasn't that simple. Why I couldn't just go in there and metaphorically poke my tongue at the admissions board and leave. That wasn't what smart girls were supposed to do. I wanted to point out that *some* people didn't have the time or the luxury to set up in an elevator and tell people to dress in bowties for non-existent appointments. I wanted to say a lot of things but nothing would come out.

"You should probably go," she said, nodding to the door behind me. "It's going to start beeping soon."

"Right." I stepped out into a hall very similar to the one I'd left only to see a woman coming towards me beckoning impatiently. All the nausea and churning that had evaporated during our manic giggle came flooding back at the twitch of that woman's fingers.

"Hey!" called Claire. I looked over my shoulder at her. She gave the thumbs up. "Just think about it."

The door closed.

By that stage the woman had reached me. "Miss Cain?" she asked.

I barely had time to nod the affirmative before she grabbed me by the elbow and started dragging me down the hall, broken thoughts and messed up feelings trailing in my wake.

"Of all the days for the elevator to be playing up. You're on in 5mins."

You're on. Like a bloody performing dog.

Escorting me into a small boardroom with two bench tables facing each other, she indicated the last spare seat in the room and backed out, closing the door behind her. The seat was next to four other students in various states of nervousness. One boy looked so green I swore he was going to puke. The girl next to me narrowed her eyes as though sizing up an opponent. On the table opposite us were two balding men and a woman in a wrinkled suit with her hair cut in a chin length bob. I'm assuming to avoid showing up the hairless men. None of them paid the slightest attention to us, flicking through documents or browsing their phones with bored expressions.

I pulled out the squeaky chair and sat, a million thoughts vying for prominence, but one question kept bubbling to the surface. *Was it really that simple?*

My thoughts were interrupted by the board woman trilling, "Welcome, welcome!" The woman stood, only managing to give herself an extra foot or two of height. "Congratulations on choosing the University of Adelaide, one of Australia's premier institutions for your higher education. We only take the best and the brightest in this accelerated course. You have to be brave, smart and willing to work under extreme pressure to achieve your dream. Not all of you will make it from the interviews today, but that doesn't spell the end, we've dozens of degrees to choose from in your end-of-year applications! Today, we'll be giving you a mix of ethical, exploratory and creative questions to see how you think, feel and deal with modern-day problems and scenarios. Your answers will tell us if this is the right course for you. Let's start in alphabetical order."

She looked down, riffling through some pages while I resisted the urge to puke.

"Ah! Is there a Miss Cain here?" she asked, looking up.

I raised my hand.

She smiled. "Excellent! Tell me Miss Cain. What would you do with a million ping-pong balls?"

I stared at her. *You have got to be kidding. If that's a frequent modern-*

day problem then I'm a double headed llama, I thought. *What the hell kind of question is that?*

"It's a creative question," the woman hinted with a patronising smile.

I bit back a retort of, *obviously.* Clearly this interview was set on becoming my own private Vietnam. Looking at the expressions of the other four I was certain we'd all spontaneously combust at any moment. This was so... *stupid.* What was I doing here?

"Any time now, Miss Cain."

Screw it, I thought, *I needed this about as much as a fish needs a dress. Maybe it is that simple.*

So I gave the first dumb answer that popped into my head. "I'd sell them on ebay and use the money to fund my holiday to Vegas."

The student next to me choked on her mouthful of water and another smothered a snort. The admissions board had identical hit-by-a-bus faces, all slack-jawed and stunned. Yet all of the tension and worry and confusion I'd been hugging like an anaconda for the past fortnight drained away, leaving me light and carefree. It was absolute bliss!

With great skill and precision I managed to answer every question thrown at me with one word or phrase. A feat of skill and creativity that was lost on the board. Yes. No. Absolutely. Fish-products.

When they asked me about my ambitions I responded with, "To lead a less boring life." When they asked me to tell them about myself I made up an acoustic 'Madeline' poem. I gave the bare minimum I needed to leave a bad impression without getting kicked out of the room. Because hey, I have some standards, even when failing.

At the very least I can say I gifted every other student in that room with normal facial colouring and supreme confidence. Because even if they felt inadequate, or nervous, or unimaginative, at least they were doing better than the elephant in the room.

Upon the interview's conclusion I thanked the board for a 'jolly good show' and strode from the room with a spring in my step. The whispered voice of the girl who'd sat next to me followed me out the room, "What a quack."

I didn't bother explaining myself. She didn't matter, none of them mattered. Assuming I had alienated the board enough I had just assured myself almost three extra months to get my act together. It was worth the snide remarks. With that much time up my sleeve how could I fail to come up with the perfect solution?

I bounced on the balls of my feet as a dozen of us waited for the elevator, all students from various interview rooms for the accelerated degrees of different faculties. Every so often I'd catch a sideways glance from one of the students who'd been in my room. I can only imagine their thoughts at the faces I made in return.

Having been almost an hour since I first came up I didn't expect Claire to be in the elevator when the door opened. But there she was, sitting on the desk, her little legs primly crossed and a pair of fake spectacles on her nose.

"Ah, come in, come in!" she said as the students shuffled through the door. "I suppose you're all wondering why I've gathered you here today…"

What I would've given to have had a video camera to capture the faces of those poor souls as Claire gave a 40 second lecture on school 'rules' to the trapped audience.

"There is to be no planking. No chewing gum traps. No bobsledding down the staircases. All University guests must be called 'Your Eminence' and the Chancellor is always to be called 'Master'. If you're asked to stand in as his coffee table, you do it. You're not to bring pets onto campus, this includes imaginary pets such as pet unicorns and pet giant caterpillars. And absolutely NO albino chimpanzees. I can't stress that one enough."

I was almost disappointed when the elevator dinged and the doors shuddered open. I stepped out into the hallway and straight into the stomach of a security guard. A rotund man almost three feet taller than me, he was hard to miss. It was easy to guess why he was there, but I was in too good a mood to let him spoil it.

"I think the girl you're looking for is that one," I said to him, pointing at the overdressed, sour-faced girl who called me a quack. "She's been in there for hours, demanding appointments, hounding students. It would be alright but she's horrible at telling jokes."

"Right," he grunted. "Thanks."

I grinned and sidled past him, confident Claire would see the opportunity I'd created and grab it.

Sure enough as I stepped out into the sunlight and stretched, tilting my face up to soak in those sweet rays of freedom, a petite figure pulled up next to me.

"Thanks," said Claire, stubbing a toe into the ground.

"Pleasure," I replied with a grin. "What was all that elevator stuff about anyway?"

She moved in step beside me as we made our way around the back of Bonythan Hall towards North Terrace.

"Oh that old thing?" She shrugged. "It was part of my 365 Days of Fun. The appointments and the 'meeting' were just two of nine hilariously weird things you can do to people in an elevator. I thought I'd make a day of it. My favourite was calling out 'Group Hug' and then enforcing it."

"When you say 365 days, you mean…"

"Yep, a whole year of silliness. Signing up for an exchange was part of it. Things were getting too serious at home, just making it from one day to the next, that's not life. You've got to take pleasure in living, it makes all the other stuff worthwhile. At the very least it's something to look forward to every day."

"Something to look forward to each day would be nice," I sighed. "The stress is winding me up so tight I'm afraid I'll snap and go on a rampage, rhino style."

"By the way you're Wizard of Oz-ing up this path I'd have thought it had already snapped."

I flushed. "I may have told the admissions board what I'd do with their million ping-pong balls."

"Ha! I bet you did! Good on you, now you've got time to do things your way."

"Or your way!" I shot back, giving her shoulder a nudge.

She nudged me right back, grinning. "That's fine by me, sounds like you need a bit of organised fun. I've got an opening for Partner in Fun for tomorrow. And next week. And… well, basically, I need someone to take up the position for the next six weeks. If you're interested."

I hit the pedestrian-crossing button to cover my silence, pretending interest in the large green metal leaves littering the side of David Jones. "Oh, I don't know, I should really be taking the extra time to figure out what the hell I'm going to do."

"Pish-posh! One piece of fun every day gets those creative juices flowing. If you don't have something to break up all that intense thinking you'll end up making horrible life choices, like becoming a teacher and being trapped in school forever. I really don't think teachers think that through."

I snorted. But she was right. I didn't want to end up in another interview situation, who knew where I'd tell them to shove their ping-pong balls the second time around?

"Alright, you're on," I said, sealing the deal with a high-five.

Thus begins my own six weeks of fun! Now to practise my I'm-so-upset-I-didn't-win face to make sure the 'rents and teachers don't find out I threw the interview on purpose. You're all sworn to secrecy by the way. If any of you breathe a word to any adult in authority I will dress you as a lettuce and feed you to rabbits. It will be a very slow death…

[Comment . Like . Share]

Adam Goldam and **7 others** like this.

Kathy Bloomingdale No this isn't fair! How can Irish Kathy be funnier than me? I can't compete against a whole year of fun. How am I going to hold my place in your heart against such a seductive accent? *Posted Saturday 10th September at 18:04* [Comment . Like]

> **Kathy Bloomingdale** P.S. I'm surprised you made it as far as the interview. I thought for sure you'd see reason before then. I guess I owe you $5, Tim. Though Maddie did throw the interview half way through so I feel I only owe you half that. *Posted Saturday 10th September at 18:08* [Comment . Like]

Tim Gleeve I think you'll find you owe me five *euros*, being in Ireland and all. The bet was she'd go to the interview, and regardless of whether or not she decided to throw sense out the window and advocate human test subjects, she did stay until the end. Ergo, the full five euros in payment, none of this halvsies nonsense. *Posted Saturday 10th September at 18:15* [Comment . Like]

Mike Cain Anyone, and I mean anyone (Irish Kathy, Maddie, the bus driver, the woman at the corner store with an eye patch) is funnier than you Kathy. Sorry to break it to you over pixels, but it's better you hear it from me than from some Irish git who no longer wants to have 'crack' with you because of your lack of funny bone. *Posted Saturday 10th September at 18:20* [Comment . Like]

Madeline Cain You guys were *betting* on me?? Since when did one of my future career options become racehorse? *Posted Saturday 10th September at 18:24* [Comment . Like]

Tim Gleeve It's less racehorse and more rodeo horse. Will she or won't she buck this cowboy and trampled him into the dirt? You know, the kind of betting that relies less on speed and more on good old-fashion erratic unpredictability. *Posted Saturday 10th September at 18:26* [Comment . Like]

Madeline Cain Gee, thanks. I'll remember that next time you want me to pretend to be the jealous girlfriend on your dates with the clueless girls of Adelaide High. *Posted Saturday 10th September at 18:27* [Comment . Like]

TimGleeve Clearly fate got a little bit muddled today, offering you some crack rather than myself. I will have to remedy the situation by joining in *all of the crack*. Unlike you I shall revel in it, bath in it and shave with it. We'll have so much crack Adelaide won't know what hit them. Bring on the next six weeks! *Posted Saturday 10th September at 18:38* [Comment . Like]

Tim Gleeve Correction, except for tomorrow. According to my mother I can't partake in crack until I've cleaned my room. That's going to require a full day and a diving suit. Diving suits have rubber gloves right? *Posted Saturday 10th September at 18:42* [Comment . Like]

Mike Cain That's one liberal Mum ? *Posted Saturday 10th September at 18:43* [Comment . Like]

Isabelle Haigh And one bacteria-filled room. *Posted Saturday 10th September at 18:44* [Comment . Like]

Tim Gleeve She has her moments. This is not one of them. *Posted Saturday 10th September at 18:44* [Comment . Like]

Kathy Bloomingdale *Facepalm* No wonder the cute guy in room 203 won't look me in the eye anymore. At the welcome dinner he said with that sexy accent, "Up for some good crack tonight, love?" To which I replied, "Do I look like I do drugs?" *Posted Saturday 10th September at 18:47* [Comment . Like]

Tim Gleeve Clearly you do, hair doesn't get that curly on its own. *Posted Saturday 10th September at 18:47* [Comment . Like]

Madeline Cain I probably would have followed that with a kick in the balls, so you handled the situation better than I did. This comment stream has probably landed us on several police watch lists by now. If our school undergoes a drug raid this week, I'm blaming Tim. *Posted Saturday 10th September at 18:50* [Comment . Like]

Tim Gleeve The teachers are crack suckers, you mark my words. *Posted Saturday 10th September at 18:51* [Comment . Like]

Mike Cain While your plan for one million ping-pong balls is admirable sister, I feel drawing a million angry faces on them and then dropping them from above on the unsuspecting public of Rundle Mall would be a much more rewarding experience. Either that or propel them with farts at small children. *Posted Saturday 10th September at 20:01* [Comment . Like]

> **Madeline Cain** How you and I are part of the same family I have no idea. Maybe Mum was on actual crack when she had you. *Posted Saturday 10th September at 20:14* [Comment . Like]

> **Mike Cain** Your face is a crack. *Posted Saturday 10th September at 20:16* [Comment . Like]

Madeline Cain Get out of town and leave me a unicorn! I totally won something! Me, the girl who ends up with plastic dinosaurs in Christmas bonbons and mouldy stuffed animals for lucky dip prizes. I actually won a super fancy DSLR camera! Something I would never be able to afford to buy even if I collected all my pocket money over the past seventeen years. I didn't even know I'd won it until the package arrived in the mail yesterday. Trust Mum not to remember to give me the package until now. *Posted Saturday 10th September at 21:00* [Comment . Like]

> **Kathy Bloomingdale** What?! How did you win it? *Posted Saturday 10th September at 21:15* [Comment . Like]

> **Madeline Cain** Mum promised to buy me a twelve month subscription to National Geographic if I got good grades last term. The competition was in the first magazine I got. So I used our old SLR camera, the film one, to send off a shot and here we are! *Posted Saturday 10th September at 21:18* [Comment . Like]

> **Kathy Bloomingdale** Bet your Mum thinks you want those NGs for the articles. *Posted Saturday 10th September at 21:19* [Comment . Like]

> **Madeline Cain** *Snort* probably. I just like the pretty pictures.

There are so many awesome ones, but my favourites by far are the ones taken by Jason I'Anson. If Mum let me blue-tac things to the walls I'd totally have a shrine to him right now. *Posted Saturday 10th September at 21:23* [Comment . Like]

Kathy Bloomingdale Trust you to geek out on people the rest of us couldn't pick out of a line-up. Bet the fact you have a subscription to NG has given all the teachers ideas about what you should do at Uni next year. *Posted Saturday 10th September at 21:24* [Comment . Like]

Madeline Cain Bleg! Yeah, Mum and her big mouth. With her bragging I'm surprised the teachers haven't crowned me as their Queen. *Posted Saturday 10th September at 21:25* [Comment . Like]

Mike Cain I'm not. Clearly they're minutes away from crowing me King, and to crown you Queen would just be incestuous. *Posted Saturday 10th September at 21:27* [Comment . Like]

Madeline Cain Update #1, 365 Days of Fun: Create photo evidence suggesting you went on an adventure that never happened. *Posted Sunday 11th September at 18:10* [Comment . Like]

Kathy Bloomingdale Bet you were all over that with your new fancy gadget! Did people ask you where you were from? *Posted Sunday 11th September at 18:15* [Comment . Like]

Madeline Cain Not really. Though things got a bit hairy when a policeman saw us drinking from champagne glasses. But after we flashed the bottle of apple cider all was well. *Posted Sunday 11th September at 18:18* [Comment . Like]

Tim Gleeve Non-alcoholic I'm assuming. Otherwise I need to underage drink around this cop. That explains all of those Paris pictures you posted. Or should I say 'Paris' pictures. I knew I couldn't have missed my first trip via teleporter. *Posted Sunday 11th September at 18:23* [Comment . Like]

Kathy Bloomingdale Are they up? Oh, is that Claire?? She's tiny! All she needs is pointed ears to match that pixie cut and she could be a fairy. Why haven't you friended her yet? *Posted Sunday 11th September at 18:26* [Comment . Like]

Madeline Cain What about these pictures makes you think I haven't made friends? *Posted Sunday 11th September at 18:27* [Comment . Like]

Kathy Bloomingdale Not in real life stupid, in pretend life, on Facebook. *Posted Sunday 11th September at 18:28* [Comment . Like]

Tim Gleeve It disturbs me that you're equating Facebook to life. Pretend or not. *Posted Sunday 11th September at 18:28* [Comment . Like]

Madeline Cain Claire doesn't do technology. *Posted Sunday 11th September at 18:29* [Comment . Like]

Tim Gleeve WHAT?! How can she not do technology? That's... that's sacrilege! That's like being in the crusades and not partaking in a little raping and pillaging. It's like baking a cake without gluten, dairy or sugar. Without the good stuff, it's just bread; boring, dry, and likely to mould before the week is out. *Posted Sunday 11th September at 18:33* [Comment . Like]

Madeline Cain It's not like she's a caveman. She has a mobile phone. Though... she only has it because her Mum made her. I'm pretty sure her Mum calls every day. It's like the only call Claire answers. *Posted Sunday 11th September at 18:37* [Comment . Like]

Tim Gleeve If she wasn't so cool, she'd be dead to me. *Posted Sunday 11th September at 18:38* [Comment . Like]

Tim Gleeve Heard the garbage truck screech down the street so sprinted outside to put out the bin… only to realise I had no pants on. Merry Christmas Mitcham council. *Posted Monday 12th September at 07:16* [Comment . Like]

> **Madeline Cain** Quick garbage man, Christmas has come early! Take a picture and use it for all your neighbourhood cards! *Posted Monday 12th September at 08:02* [Comment . Like]
>
> **Kathy Bloomingdale** Are we just talking long pants? Or *all* the pants? *Posted Monday 12th September at 08:10* [Comment . Like]
>
> **Kathy Bloomingdale** Hmmmmm, no answer… *Posted Monday 12th September at 08:15* [Comment . Like]
>
> **Madeline Cain** Oh my God Tim! Were you not wearing *any* pants?? What's wrong with you? Why were you walking around your family home in your birthday suit? *Posted Monday 12th September at 08:17* [Comment . Like]
>
> **Tim Gleeve** Look, when a man's parents aren't home he has urges to be free. *Posted Monday 12th September at 08:19* [Comment . Like]
>
> **Madeline Cain** This is going to come back to bite you in the jubblies one day. Then I'm going to have all the fun saying I told you so. *Posted Monday 12th September at 08:20* [Comment . Like]
>
> **Tim Gleeve** I have no fear, nothing can go wrong when you're at one with nature. *Posted Monday 12th September at 08:21* [Comment . Like]

Madeline Cain Except flashing garbage men. *Posted Monday 12th September at 08:21* [Comment . Like]

Tim Gleeve It's unfortunate. *Posted Monday 12th September at 08:21* [Comment . Like]

Wyate Yosime likes the page **The Guy Who Discovered Milk... What Was He Doing With That Cow/Goat/Sheep?** [Like]

Derek Chan Making your font type bigger so it looks like you've written more, not as good a plan in practise as it is in theory. *Posted Monday 12th September at 12:00* [Comment . Like]

Madeline Cain Dude seriously? You can *sneeze* 350 words. *Posted Monday 12th September at 12:30* [Comment . Like]

Tim Gleeve Only if you're Stephen King. *Posted Monday 12th September at 12:42* [Comment . Like]

Madeline Cain Update #2, 365 Days of Fun: Go to a pet store and buy bird seed. Then ask the clerk how long it will take the birds to grow. *Posted Monday 12th September at 16:30* [Comment . Like]

Kathy Bloomingdale And? *Posted Monday 12th September at 16:48* [Comment . Like]

Madeline Cain The answer is a confused look and a disclaimed tapped to the shelf a day later advising customers the product may not work how they think it does. *Posted Monday 12th September at 16:54* [Comment . Like]

Tim Gleeve An example of when customer service and idiot proofing goes too far. *Posted Monday 12th September at 16:57* [Comment . Like]

Tim Gleeve I'm sorry Ms. Rutledge, but I'm less motivated than your average sea cucumber. *Posted Tuesday 13th September at 14:02* [Comment . Like]

Madeline Cain Even that's too motivated. You're less motivated than a pet rock. Coming to 365 DoF after school? *Posted Tuesday 13th September at 14:20* [Comment . Like]

Tim Gleeve Better not, my lack of motivation has resulted in zero free afternoons and numbero three detentions. *Posted Tuesday 13th September at 14:25* [Comment . Like]

Madeline Cain Three? How did you go from none to three in one afternoon? *Posted Tuesday 13th September at 14:36* [Comment . Like]

Tim Gleeve Apparently jokes and not finishing your short story is unappreciated in this Nazi state, hence detention one and two. Then I tried to explain to the teacher why the writing hadn't occurred, in a very down-to-earth, open and honest way, "Writing is a matter of sitting in a room where your only companion is self-doubt. Self-doubt won today. But I'll get the bastard tomorrow."

This too was unappreciated and that's when detention three joined the party. *Posted Tuesday 13th September at 14:52* [Comment . Like]

Madeline Cain Update #3, 365 Days of Fun: Go to a major book store and leave notes to future readers in the copies of your favourite books. *Posted Tuesday 13th September at 19:00* [Comment . Like]

Kathy Bloomingdale What sorts of messages did you leave? *Posted Tuesday 13th September at 19:08* [Comment . Like]

Madeline Cain "In this book you will meet a dark stranger. He is not important. But the broomstick might be." "Make sure you're wearing a wreath of garlic before you read on." "Help me! Help me! Arghldasjfgosduvs Oh no, you weren't in time to stop the murder, I guess you'll have to solve it." "This is my favourite book of all time. If you hate it, we can never, ever be friends." And other assorted messages. *Posted Tuesday 13th September at 19:14* [Comment . Like]

Tim Gleeve If you reveal that Darth Vader is Luke's father, some future nerd is going to be very unhappy with you. *Posted Tuesday 13th September at 19:16* [Comment . Like]

Mike Cain I would have told them Dumbledore dies. *Posted Tuesday 13th September at 19:22* [Comment . Like]

Mike Cain Oooh, then I would have gotten a Goosebumps book and told them just by opening to the first page, they'd released a monster into their house. *Posted Tuesday 13th September at 19:26* [Comment . Like]

Mike Cain Then I would have opened any chick-lit novel and written, 'She's going to marry that prick'. *Posted Tuesday 13th September at 19:29* [Comment . Like]

Madeline Cain Book store, not movie store, Tim. That's why I would never, ever bring you along with me on these fun dates, Mike. Deep down in your very core, you're too evil. *Posted Tuesday 13th September at 19:37* [Comment . Like]

Mike Cain Finally, in the Christmas books, I would have told them Santa isn't real and there is only Jesus. Not that I give a flying fart in space about religion. I'd do it just so I could frame a priest. *Posted Tuesday 13th September at 19:40* [Comment . Like]

Mike Cain I wanna perform for an all-gay crowd so I can thank everyone in the audience for coming out. *Posted Wednesday 14th September at 11:04* [Comment . Like]

Madeline Cain Are you sure that's the *only* reason? *Posted Wednesday 14th September at 13:07* [Comment . Like]

Of Tarot Cards & Strangers – 365 Days of Fun

NOTES > **My Notes** [Write a note]

By **Madeline Cain**. Wednesday, 14 September 2011 at 20:00.

Have you ever had the urge to tell a stranger they would die in a freak, gasoline fight accident? Or a child that they will bring about the apocalypse? Or vaguely intone to a well-dressed woman that even the most charming of wallflowers wither and die, unless they're forced to grow in other directions? Or tell your teacher that they would fall through their neighbour's skylight dressed as a fairy?

Well you can do all that and more if you set up as a fortune teller in Mosely Square at Glenelg Beach. Go off your nut with as many crazed predictions as your mind can conjure. Goodness knows Claire and I did, and as a result of our mysterious connection to the veils beyond I can safely say we have made Adelaide a more confused and paranoid place. You're welcome Radelaidians.

I don't think I've laughed this hard in twelve months, not since the dark shadow of year twelve descended to strangle us (well, me). If I'd known all it would take was one joke tarot pack, I'd have been peddling my fortune telling powers long before this.

When I arrived Claire had already set up to one side of the pioneer memorial facing the square and the tram stop. A brilliant blue sky was her back drop complimented by the lush grass that led you to the sand beyond. A path wandered from the desk she set up to the Glenelg Pier jutting out across the water. The sun was already making preparations to set in an hour or two so I had to squint to make out the sign hanging from the table.

Apprentice fortune tellers. Get your free reading now!

I weaved my way through shoppers and kids on their after-school jaunts to get to the table, finding Claire already occupied with a 'customer'.

"Hmmm, these cards are telling me many things. You have a scar on your knee... and there are some photos in your house that have never been organised... in your draw there's a key which unlocks... well, you're not sure." Claire cocked her head, sweeping a hand dramatically over four cards laid in a grid.

"That's all a bit, vague isn't it?" asked the woman, flicking her mousy brown hair over her shoulder.

"Just getting comfortable with the spread. The images are coming faster now. I see an albino dwarf taking up residence in your stomach. It'll be a bit uncomfortable at times, but he will help with your rent. How interesting, I see you wearing a Marilyn Monroe wig while stroking your monkey. And..."

Claire frowned and looked up, making the woman squirm.

"Uh, I'm not sure of that last image... it could be a hamster." Claire shrugged. "You should probably be careful of them or something. I hope the rest of your day is hamster free."

The woman blinked at her for several seconds before finally standing and stalking off.

"What is it with you and albinos?" I asked, flopping myself into the seat beside her.

She grinned, leaning down to pull a book out of her back pack. "They just call to me. I'm glad you're here, I didn't want to pull this out until you arrived. I've been making things up until now. It's hard work!"

She put down the book and swept up the four cards shoving them at the bottom of a card deck and weighing them down with a rock. The book was pretty simple, just a black paperback with silver writing and a lot of gold stars scattered across the cover like confetti. The title was, 'Funny Tarot, A Mystical Guide To Confusing The Hell Out Of People'.

"Let's see if it works." Claire wiggled her eyebrows at me.

Shooting her hand into the air, Claire waved at a young guy

shuffling slowly across the square on crutches. "Sir! Excuse me sir! Would you like to know your future for free?"

I was convinced he'd ignore us and keep walking. But instead he hesitated, looked left then right then shrugged and changed direction towards our table.

He flicked an untidy fringe out of his eyes and said, "My mate's ten minutes late anyway, so what the hell. You a gypsy or something?"

"I don't follow," Claire said, shuffling the deck and swearing under her breath as several cards escaped.

"I just thought, you know, the accent."

Claire tapped her nose. "Ah yes, yes indeed I am a gypsy, from the emerald isle. Very astute. Now if you could please cut the deck in two and pick three cards and then flip them over in a line from left to right. These cards will represent your past, present and future."

The young man considered the cards for a second, then looking Claire straight in the eye he picked up the top quarter of the pack, and pulled out three cards laying them purposefully in the wrong order. Claire continued to smile politely at him as he pretended to fuss over setting the deck straight and weighing it back down.

Poor unsuspecting sod, he didn't know that regardless of where he took those cards from, this reading was going to be about as accurate as an archer with a blind fold.

"The cards you've flipped are The Sun, for the Past, Death for the Present and Two of Cups for the Future," Claire intoned opening the book and flicking through the first couple of pages. "All of the cards you've flipped…" She left the sentence hanging, casting an expectant look in his direction.

"Chad," he replied with a smirk.

"All the cards you've flipped, Chad, have been placed in *normal* positions. Now this could mean your life isn't particularly interesting, *or* that you just can't seem to stop telling everyone to go to hell. A string of marvellous things may or may not happen but I'm leaning towards them not since you seem to be pissing so many people off."

"Hey now," Chad said, holding up his hands. "Maybe we got off on the wrong foot. Why don't we try doing this properly-"

"Oh no, the spread has already been laid out. We must continue."

Claire, face serious, laid her hand over his and moved it away from the cards. She picked up the book and flicked several more pages with a flourish. "The Sun card tells me your past was filled with much happiness. There was always enough time to sneak into the male locker room and take pictures of nude men in the showers."

"Hey that's not-"

Claire's voice continued over his like a steamroller. "However, this was not without some hurdles. You were caught countless times by the cops for running through the city with men's knickers on your head landing you with the name the Skid-mark Kid, or Skid-kid, for the rest of your life."

"Hey Skid-kid," I said, wiggling my eyebrows.

"Come on, that's not even remotely-"

"Aha!" Claire paused on the next relevant page. "In the here and now the Death card tells me there's change a foot. Whether you will change from being a disliked person to a vaguely tolerated person, or into some other non-humanoid-pubic-hair-monster, we may never know. But what we do know is that since sitting down for this reading there is the distinct possibility you now have the power to control the minds of small animals."

Chad snorted and crossed his arms. "Really? Then I'd command the birds to-"

Claire raised her voice. "This is obviously a very mild super power, but it may back-fire and end up with your leg getting gnawed off by a snake or a platypus so just be careful. Now finally, to the future!"

I ducked as Claire flung her pale arms wide almost braining me with the book.

In dramatic tones she said, "Two of Cups dictates your future and tells me that after years of painting your toenails red and dressing up in your mother's clothing that you're finally ready to come out to everybody..."

"What the heck-" The Skid-kid struggled to standing position but Claire was like a train that couldn't be stopped.

"-Come out to everyone as an elephant trainer and put this whole naked-men-dirty-underwear-fetish behind you. Maybe one day you'll even use your elephants to demolish your family home so no one can ever steal your sweet childhood memories from you via property redevelopment."

"Look, this has gone a little weird-"

"You'll marry the first elephant you ever trained and it will be a glorious affair that will only be trumped by your induction into the Circus Hall of Fame for breaking all four limbs after being trampled by your elephant wife-"

"-I'm leaving now. You loonies have fun." Chad snatched up his crutches and split.

"But Skid-Kid," called Claire after the hobbling figure. "Don't you want to know how you die? It's a doozy!"

I wiped tears from my eyes as Claire twirled and took a bow.

"What did I tell you? This book is comedy gold!" she said.

It took ten minutes before someone approached our table again, but we put that ten minutes to good use with costume prep, donning curly haired wigs, patterned bandanas, and layers of fake pendants and jewels.

"Ooooh, prospective victim at twelve o'clock," whispered Claire as a middle-aged woman with dark brown hair walked slowly towards our table. Claire thumped me on the back. "You're on!"

Raising her voice Claire said, "Why hello young lady! Would you like a three day forecast to help ease your mind? The cards have been most accurate today."

"Most accurate my arse," I muttered.

The woman looked hesitantly towards the beach. Clearly we'd misinterpreted her direction in our eagerness for another subject to confuse. The woman glanced at her watch and shrugged. "Sure, that sounds fun." She was quite soft spoken and had the habit of smoothing imaginary wrinkles from her bird patterned dress.

She sat down. The woman and Claire looked at me expectantly and it took me a moment to remember that I was supposed to be running the show. I wiped my suddenly sweaty palms on my shorts. This was a lot more nerve wracking than Claire made it look, especially now I knew the sorts of predictions I was likely to be reading out.

"Right. You ah, you pick up these cards, and shuffle them, and ah, divide them into three and take one card from the top of each pile."

Claire nodded encouragingly as the woman did my bidding flipping over three cards. One had a large, medieval looking sword with nine smaller swords around it, the middle one had nine golden cups with blue jewels in rows of three, and the final was one very flamboyantly dressed man with luscious locks, captioned 'The Emperor'.

I tapped my lips, hoping it made me look more thoughtful. "Right. Ok. Right. So for tomorrow you have the... the ten of swords, and for Friday it's the nine of cups and Saturday is Fabio the Emperor."

I cracked open the book flicking past the page for the ten of swords twice before finding it. I took a deep breath and dived in.

"The **ten of swords** signifies you have the readiness to deal with most things tomorrow. Which is handy because within the next twenty-four hours your encounters will include a strange pink elephant who burps fairy floss and wears ducks as slippers, and your next-door neighbour convincing himself that his children are Angry Birds. This will result in him launching them via a giant sling shot through your bedroom window."

I chanced a glance at the woman. Her expression was a comical mix of deer-in-the-headlights and play-it-cool-you're-being-punked which resulted in wild eyes and crazed half-smile.

I knew better than to look at Claire.

"Now to Friday." I flipped furiously through the pages. "The Nine of Cups is quite specific. You will find yourself inexplicably drawn to your neighbour's kid's twelfth birthday party in order to lecture them on the dangers of butterflies and the stupidity of bring a paintball gun to school and taking your sports teacher hostage. You give them the age old advice to just kicking anything they don't like in the balls. Later, you will find yourself awaiting bail for streaking down the street wearing nothing but a newspaper."

The woman by this time had substituted her card gazing for staring at me, her horrified look only flaring the red flush I could feel spreading across my cheeks. Claire's poorly suppressed squeaks from stage-right were only making it harder to keep a straight face.

My voice pitched higher and higher as I barrelled forth to the final page and the end. "On Saturday, you will be faced with a terrible decision. Will you bake blueberry muffins and throw them at the stray neighbourhood cats or will you put on some pants? Frankly, people need to stay out of your business Saturday. Your lady bits don't concern them. You might need to keep a brick in your handbag just in case you need to smash faces during those twenty-four hours. By the next morning you'll awaken lain over a tree limb. While you'll be unable to remember what happened between all that Citrus Vodka and the naked volleyball session on your front lawn, you *do* have an inkling that you neighbours may be a little pissed at you and you have a lot of explaining to do."

My red-faced silence was filled by a sound not dissimilar to a dying whoopee-cushion as Claire completely lost her shit. The woman took a moment to unfreeze, but then she was up, smoothing down her dress once again and fumbling to pick up her beach bag.

"Well then..." She trailed off, edging away. "That was educational."

"Thank you for your time," I managed, throwing in a cheeky wave.

It may be of no surprise to you that I handed the reins to Claire after that. Holding in that much laughter was threatening to burst all the organs I held dear. So instead I gave myself stitches from afar by using the long lens of my fancy new camera to record the event, and customer facial expressions for those who were unable to drop their load in person (I'm looking at you Leprechaun Kathy, Detention Tim). I ended up with some very specy photos if I do say so myself. Even a photograph of a turd is made golden by this camera.

It's been a while since I invented things for the fun of it, and now I can't even think how I let myself stop in the first place. Less than a week in, I can already tell that 365 Days of Fun is going to be my sanity blanket for the rest of the year. When your mind starts conjuring possibilities for the next weird thing you can do to trigger that look of mild panic on the face of strangers, you know you're hooked.

I shall conclude this psychological (psychic-ological?) experiment slash post with a sage prophecy from our favourite Tarot book (yes, this book also has prophecies, palm reading guides and my favourite, suggested one-sided conversations with the dead).

When in doubt, consider who can be blamed if you f*** it up.

[Comment . Like . Share]

Lulu Tanaki and **9 others** like this.

Tim Gleeve I'd be more than happy with an elephant who burps fairy-floss and wears duck slippers! If it could poop M&Ms it'd be a triple win. You girls can read for me any time. Those future insights are a hundred and eleven percent better than the vague pronouncements of Mr Flynn in his 'future booth' at school carnival last year: "Generally you dislike pain." "When you were a child you were much shorter." *Posted Wednesday 14th September at 20:20* [Comment . Like]

> **Madeline Cain** I remember that! "You will take a trip...to the next suburb over." *Posted Wednesday 14th September at 20:25* [Comment . Like]

> **Tim Gleeve** "Sometimes you are cheery, other times you are not..." *Posted Wednesday 14th September at 20:27* [Comment . Like]

> **Madeline Cain** "You will get married... sometime before you die." *Posted Wednesday 14th September at 20:28* [Comment . Like]

> **Tim Gleeve** If only he'd gotten more specific and told the kids faking a sicky that he was sending an albino dwarf into their stomach for a diagnosis. Then he may have finally attained that level of coolness he was striving for. *Posted Wednesday 14th September at 20:31* [Comment . Like]

> **Madeline Cain** Or told them their fate was going to be decided

by a hamster. *Posted Wednesday 14th September at 20:32* [Comment . Like]

Tim Gleeve Frankly, everyone's fate should be decided by a hamster. It's the logical way forward. *Posted Wednesday 14th September at 20:33* [Comment . Like]

Kathy Bloomingdale I'm not sure how sanity-inducing this project is, it sounds to me like it's your *insanity* blanket for the rest of the year. Forget apprentice fortune teller, you two are apprentice trouble makers. Whatever you do don't tell your Mum! I can hear her now: "If you put as much time into your education as you do dreaming up schemes, you'd be a doctor." Actually, I'm pretty sure I've heard her say that several times already. But to Mike. *Posted Wednesday 14th September at 20:43* [Comment . Like]

> **Madeline Cain** Don't go comparing me to my crazed brother. He does this so he has a portfolio for entry into Evil Genius University. I do it to let off steam and beat back the frustration of staring into the distance and seeing nothing but fog in my future. Probably due to a butt-ton of ghost hamsters. *Posted Wednesday 14th September at 20:46* [Comment . Like]

> **Kathy Bloomingdale** Mhmm, or perhaps to avoid condensing those foggy ghost animals into an attainable goal? *Posted Wednesday 14th September at 20:47* [Comment . Like]

> **Madeline Cain** How is it you can see into my deepest, darkest soul? *Posted Wednesday 14th September at 20:48* [Comment . Like]

> **Kathy Bloomingdale** I still maintain we were fraternal twins separated at birth. Take that Claire! *Posted Wednesday 14th September at 20:49* [Comment . Like]

> **Madeline Cain** No need to be jealous, you're still the one I

come to for advice. *Posted Wednesday 14th September at 20:51* [Comment . Like]

Derek Chan Why does no one else seem as disturbed as I am by the image of a pubic-hair monster? *Gag.* *Posted Wednesday 14th September at 20:55* [Comment . Like]

> **Tim Gleeve** I prefer to focus on the image of my neighbour dressing his children as Angry Birds and shooting them from slingshots. They deserve it, I'm certain at least one of them is the Anti-Christ. *Posted Wednesday 14th September at 20:58* [Comment . Like]

> **Madeline Cain** Just imagine holding Mr Carney hostage with a paintball gun. That should brighten your day. *Posted Wednesday 14th September at 20:59* [Comment . Like]

Mike Cain Pffft, you guys need someone like me on the team, I can make up fortunes with my eyes closed, hanging upside down in a vat of honey, with my nuts up near my kidneys. Check this out: "In the next year, it's quite possible you'll become one of two things, either the manager of a kindergarten or a brigadier on a Somalian pirate ship. Either way you'll be dealing with people who think with their swords." *Self high-five.* *Posted Wednesday 14th September at 21:13* [Comment . Like]

> **Madeline Cain** That's the most disturbing image I've ever had thrust upon me. I hereby un-invite you to any 365 Day of Fun activities Future-Madeline was going to invite you to. Honey on toast will never be the same again. *Posted Wednesday 14th September at 21:18* [Comment . Like]

> **Tim Gleeve** Now you've put me off my breakfast. *Posted Wednesday 14th September at 21:20* [Comment . Like]

> **Kathy Bloomingdale** I'd be careful if I were you, Mike, you're the original Skid-kid. Turn too many people off their breakfasts

and I'm sure those photos can be found... *Posted Wednesday 14th September at 21:22* [Comment . Like]

Mike Cain Why ya gotta ruin these brainstorming sessions and make things personal? *Posted Wednesday 14th September at 21:23* [Comment . Like]

Madeline Cain She's just trying to save you from getting trampled by an elephant wife. *Posted Wednesday 14th September at 21:24* [Comment . Like]

Virginia Lowe I feel like the life lesson from this is that South Australian Bogans will believe anything. Next time you should put out a donation box, at least that way a charity will benefit from their superstitious beliefs. *Posted Wednesday 14th September at 21:35* [Comment . Like]

Tim Gleeve I feel like the key lesson from today is that as soon as you start throwing blueberry muffins at cats, it's a short, slippery slope to Citrus Vodka and naked volleyball. *Posted Wednesday 14th September at 21:39* [Comment . Like]

Kathy Bloomingdale I had a dream last night that I was visiting Iceland. I think the cold may be getting to me. *Posted Thursday 15th September at 06:52* [Comment . Like]

Tim Gleevc Tell the truth now, you've been on the Guinness before your birthday, haven't you? It's giving you kooky dreams. *Posted Thursday 15th September at 07:55* [Comment . Like]

Madeline Cain If she had, she'd have hair on the chest and the cold, clearly, would not be getting to her. *Posted Thursday 15th September at 08:00* [Comment . Like]

Madeline Cain Update #5, 365 Days of Fun: Messy Twister – cover twister dots in paint and play. *Posted Thursday 15th September at 16:30* [Comment . Like]

> **Tim Gleeve** Now I look like that guy out of Braveheart. *Posted Thursday 15th September at 16:40* [Comment . Like]

> **Madeline Cain** At least you don't have a hand print on your butt. *Posted Thursday 15th September at 16:42* [Comment . Like]

> **Kathy Bloomingdale** Tim! *Posted Thursday 15th September at 16:43* [Comment . Like]

> **Tim Gleeve** Don't look at me! Irish Kathy has about as much balance as a drunk penguin. *Posted Thursday 15th September at 16:44* [Comment . Like]

> **Madeline Cain** The question is, when will Claire finally snap and deck you for continuing to call her Irish Kathy? *Posted Thursday 15th September at 16:47* [Comment . Like]

> **Tim Gleeve** The questions is, why won't this paint wash off?! *Posted Thursday 15th September at 16:49* [Comment . Like]

Kate Nikle likes the pages **It's Ok Pluto, I'm Not A Planet Either** and **Procrastinators UNITE... Tomorrow...** [Like]

Tim Gleeve Watching the Doomsday Preppers. Seriously, if it comes to 'Let's drink our own pee' then I'm happy for the zombies to eat me. *Posted Thursday 15th September at 19:30* [Comment . Like]

> **Madeline Cain** I'm happy with that, you can act as bait while I run away. And when I'm safe I'll carbonate that pee and drink it like champagne. Sucker. *Posted Thursday 15th September at 19:45* [Comment . Like]

> **Tim Gleeve** Read that reply again, consider it like a normal

person and then tell me who the sucker really is. *Posted Thursday 15th September at 19:50* [Comment . Like]

Madeline Cain Update #6, 365 Days of Fun: Text 'I hid the body' to a random number. *Posted Friday 16th September at 16:47* [Comment . Like]

> **Kathy Bloomingdale** From your phone? *Posted Friday 16th September at 16:47* [Comment . Like]
>
> **Madeline Cain** Of course not. From an old phone we bought at Cash Converters. It's very easy to buy a cheap SIM these days... *Posted Friday 16th September at 16:54* [Comment . Like]
>
> **Kathy Bloomindale** Are you in the middle of a Freaky Friday, body snatch scenario with your brother right now? This is really Mike, isn't it? *Posted Friday 16th September at 17:10* [Comment . Like]
>
> **Mike Cain** I wish! Best idea ever! Why are you cutting me out, sis? *Posted Friday 16th September at 17:20* [Comment . Like]
>
> **Madeline Cain** Because you'd reply to the guy who texted back: "Wrong number, mate. No need to come after me, I'm not a snitch. But if you do, just be aware I've raised Geese who are trained to go for the soft bits. You've been warned." *Posted Friday 16th September at 17:22* [Comment . Like]

Mike Cain Me: Oh babe! You've got a pimple!

Mandy: ...Yep.

Me: I feel like I've made a mistake.

Posted Friday 16th September at 18:20 [Comment . Like]

> **Madeline Cain** Ha! Tim owes me $5. Told him this one

wouldn't last the week. *Posted Friday 16th September at 18:36* [Comment . Like]

Tim Gleeve I had too much faith in her hotness. *Posted Friday 16th September at 18:40* [Comment . Like]

Kathy Bloomingdale You just called a thirteen year old girl hot. *Posted Friday 16th September at 18:43* [Comment . Like]

Tim Gleeve My fingers are possessed. I'm not responsible for their output. *Posted Friday 16th September at 18:45* [Comment . Like]

Tim Gleeve likes the page **When My Bowling Ball Is Rolling I Try To Use The Force To Strike!** [Like]

Ray Star It's alarming to learn that nurses refuse to touch a drug that you've been casually breaking in two for your wife for years. *Posted Friday 16th September at 20:39* [Comment . Like]

Lulu Tanaki I was wondering why you had no hands. *Posted Friday 16th September at 20:45* [Comment . Like]

Ray Star Helpful. Imuran is apparently psychotoxic. At least I wasn't licking it. *Posted Friday 16th September at 20:48* [Comment . Like]

Madeline Cain Just stick with the toad licking. Possibly safer for all. *Posted Friday 16th September at 20:53* [Comment . Like]

Lulu Tanaki We keep the toads in the Occult Magic cupboard, right next to the Controlled Drug cupboard. Noisy buggers they are too. *Posted Friday 16th September at 20:54* [Comment . Like]

Madeline Cain Especially during full moon right? *Posted Friday 16th September at 20:55* [Comment . Like]

Lulu Tanaki Actually the toads get spookily quiet on the full moon. It's the patients that go haywire. *Posted Friday 16th September at 20:56* [Comment . Like]

Kathy Bloomingdale When my aunt was on Imuran I touched it and it wasn't an issue. Though her specialist did say for her not to pee on any family members. Personally, I'd like to know the story behind why he gives *that* disclaimer… *Posted Friday 16th September at 20:59* [Comment . Like]

Kathy Bloomingdale I think my phone is on crack. 81 degrees Celsius (aka 177 Fahrenheit)? Uh, no. *Posted Friday 16th September at 22:11* [Comment . Like]

Madeline Cain I think your phone is getting ready to self-destruct. Did you get a suspicious email marked, 'Top Secret'? Run away, run away! (To my house…. For dinner…) *Posted Friday 16th September at 22:40* [Comment . Like]

Kathy Bloomingdale Sorry, can't. Being a whole ocean away and all that. *Posted Friday 16th September at 22:43* [Comment . Like]

Madeline Cain Pft. Fine. You should probs still run away from the exploding phone. *Posted Friday 16th September at 22:44* [Comment . Like]

Kathy Bloomingdale Yeah. Probs. *Posted Friday 16th September at 22:46* [Comment . Like]

Virginia Lowe Our lives begin to end the day we become silent about things that matter. *Posted Saturday 17th September at 10:14* [Comment . Like]

Tim Gleeve In that case, I think it's time to pass a bill outlawing socks and boat sandals (Aka German Tourist Shoes). All offenders should be shot on sight for crimes against my eyes.

Phew! I feel more alive already. *Posted Saturday 17th September at 11:20* [Comment . Like]

Kyle Traybna So much for the Neverending Story never ending. *Posted Saturday 17th September at 13:30* [Comment . Like]

Madeline Cain After eight months of agonising and a further two months of ignoring everything remotely related to future career paths, I've had a brain fart. Which is either a hopeful story of opportunity or a sign of the coming apocalypse. *Posted Saturday 17th September at 15:10* [Comment . Like]

Is It Just A Hobby? Or Can I DO Something With It? [New Message]

[Back to messages. Mark as unread . Report spam . Delete]

Between **Kathy Bloomingdale** and **You.**

———————

Madeline Cain 17 September 2011 at 15:22

I was pretending to be a marooned pirate today when Claire said something interesting. But I'm not sure if she's right. I mean, in that it could *lead* to anything. For a start, I enjoy it too much, so that automatically tells me other people probably enjoy it too and wouldn't actually *pay* someone to do it for them.

Kathy Bloomindale 17 September 2011 at 15:36 [Report]

I'm not sure you can get paid for pretending to be a pirate. Unless you're Jonny Depp, but that requires a dedication to the acting profession and actually being good at lying. And I'm sorry to say, pretending to be someone other than you is not your forte. It's like watching animated cardboard.

Sorry, I know it's fun, I do, I've tried it myself. But I hope you don't have your heart set on being a pirate. For pretend, that is. If you're talking about doing it for real it's less about getting paid and more about finding someone to raid.

Madeline Cain 17 September 2011 at 15:38

What the hell are you talking about?

Kathy Bloomingdale 17 September 2011 at 15:42 [Report]

Me? What are *you* talking about?? You're the one going on about being a marooned pirate and speculating whether someone would pay you to do it. I just linked the logical sentences.

Madeline Cain 17 September 2011 at 15:43

I don't see how you could have... oh wait, I see where that came from. No, the pirate comment was a separate component to the rest of the ranting stream of consciousness.

Kathy Bloomingdale 17 September 2011 at 15:45 [Report]

Let me take a moment to re-align the gears then. Before we continue with the D&M, can you tell me why you were pretending to be a marooned pirate? I need a study break from all the costume crazy that's invaded my brain.

Madeline Cain 17 September 2011 at 15:45

Do you want to talk about it?

Kathy Bloomingdale 17 September 2011 at 15:46 [Report]

Nope. I want to fill my head with visions of marooned pirates. Now go!

Madeline Cain 17 September 2011 at 15:48

This probably isn't the epic you were hoping for but ok... Claire and I were throwing messages in a bottle from the Henley Beach pier. In our messages we claimed to be pirates Rogers and Periwinkle, marooned on a not-so-desert isle with a pig, an albatross and a hidden store room of grapefruit juice.

Kathy Bloomingdale 17 September 2011 at 15:49 [Report]

What a dastardly situation! And??

Madeline Cain 17 September 2011 at 15:51

We inserted a map of Kangaroo Island, marked an X near a cliff somewhere and promised them boxes of Pop-tarts if they came and rescued us.

Kathy Bloomingdale 17 September 2011 at 15:51 [Report]

A rich and tasty reward! And???

Madeline Cain 17 September 2011 at 15:52

They are now floating in the ocean?

Kathy Bloomingdale 17 September 2011 at 15:52 [Report]

That's really it?

Madeline Cain 17 September 2011 at 15:53

Well, we dressed up as pirates too, but that was really to have an excuse to say, "Arrrg!"

Kathy Bloomingdale 17 September 2011 at 15:54 [Report]

Sigh, not the distraction I was hoping for. Why is it when you invite procrastination with open arms you only get the sound of a tiny violin?

Madeline Cain 17 September 2011 at 15:56

Wow, are you sure you're just after distraction? You don't need a reset button or something before you overheat? That may be *your* experience of procrastination, but mine has resulted in a possibly bearable future plan. I think. Maybe. At least, Claire seems to think so.

Kathy Bloomingdale 17 September 2011 at 15:57 [Report]

Face palm Of course! You have life questions you need answering, how could I forget? I blame pirates for being so shinny. Lay it on me!

Madeline Cain 17 September 2011 at 16:04

Ok, but don't think I'm not coming back to you and your crazy later.

So, we were walking to the pier in our costumes, and by costumes I mean a pirate patch, hat and fake hook. Claire was all for a wooden leg but I was... less keen. Mainly because we had to walk across a lot of sand to get there from the bus stop. I could see me eating a mouth full of sand if I tried. It was an overcast afternoon so the sea had a beautiful steel grey colour that looks awesome in photographs, all dramatic and brooding.

So I did what I normally do on a meander with friends, I stopped every time I saw something interesting and took a photo. The one difference being, I used to have Mum's film SLR camera with its finite number of shots, but now I had a device that would take *infinite photos!* I felt like I'd the power of God in my hands, and like all beings who find themselves suddenly all-powerful, I may have gotten a little overenthusiastic.

Kathy Bloomingdale 17 September 2011 at 16:05 [Report]

Even without power your whole family is the very definition of overenthusiastic.

Madeline Cain 17 September 2011 at 16:11

I'll ignore your jibe and sugar coat it for consumption as a compliment!

While you know this is a regular occurrence, particularly if I've saved up enough money to buy a roll of film, this was the first time Claire had been exposed to my give-it-a-110%-or-go knit-with-grandma policy.

After twenty minutes of constant photo taking, Claire gave a big, gusty sigh. "That's like, the millionth photo you've taken."

To be fair, that was probably an accurate estimate.

Rather than walk ahead like she had for the other 999,999 photos,

Claire planted her feet wide and put her hands on her hips. "Why all the shots? Am I missing some invisible world only viewable by Australians? Do I need to pat a koala before I can see the little sand-mermaid you're trying to photograph?"

"Sorry," I replied. I shot another sneaky photo as she cast an impatient look over her shoulder at the pier, less than a kilometre away. She turned back to me and I shrugged. "It's just something I do. I'll stop now."

Clair gave a dismissive wave. "Don't be dramatic. You don't have to stop, I just wanted to know *why*. What do you *do* with them?"

"I don't *do* anything in particular with them, they're just for me. I used to take photos with my Mum's old film camera, but you couldn't really test things. But with this bad boy..." I hefted the large camera, which is frankly big enough to knock out a baby hippo. "- With this I can start to get closer to the types of photos they put in National Geographic. Who knows, maybe with two decades of practise I can be good as Jason I'Anson."

Kathy Bloomingdale 17 September 2011 at 16:13 [Report]

Imagine being one of those professional photographers. They have cameras big enough that if you dropped them off the Empire State Building you'd probably leave a crater in the concrete.

Madeline Cain 17 September 2011 at 16:22

Um, I suppose...

To avoid the self-conscious feeling I get every time Claire employs her stare tactics I set off towards the pier again, hand glued to my head to stop the wind from force feeding me hair.

Claire fell in step, holding up a hand to shield her eyes from a shaft of bright light escaping between clouds. "Who's Jason I-what's-his-face?"

"Jason I'Anson. He's an amazeballs travel and landscape photographer.

I don't think there's been a single NG issue I have that he hasn't been in."

"I only get those for the pictures." Claire jumped over a line of pungent seaweed, her nose wrinkled.

I laughed. "Me too! It's so much fun to try re-creating them. I have a whole notebook where one page will have the actual photo, and the other page will have my best re-creation. Sometimes you have to use stuffed animals and table ornaments and things but they still turn out pretty good."

By this point we'd reached the pier and the wind was driving stinging grains of sand into our shins.

Claire bounded up the stairs two at a time. "If you love it so much," she called over her shoulder, "Why don't you study photography?"

The anvil dropped and suddenly my head was an explosion of stars.

Kathy Bloomingdale 17 September 2011 at 16:23 [Report]

What?! Someone dropped an anvil on your head??

Madeline Cain 17 September 2011 at 16:24

No! I was trying to be poetic! Metaphorical! You know, 'the penny dropped'.

So what do you think??

Kathy Bloomingdale 17 September 2011 at 16:25 [Report]

Right! Sorry, study brain. So what do I think about doing some sort of photography course, degree, thingo? I didn't even know they existed as their own thing. I thought you had to do it with arts and media degrees.

Madeline Cain 17 September 2011 at 16:27

Ah! Here's the thing, this is why I was a little weirded out by your Empire State Building reference. There is a twelve-month course at a college in New York City. They take only seven students every six months. And, would you believe, the college is owned and run by Jason?

Kathy Bloomingdale 17 September 2011 at 16:28 [Report]

Shut the front door! Are you kidding me? How did you not know about this beforehand? I feel like you'd have talked my ear off about it if you'd even the slightest hint it existed.

Madeline Cain 17 September 2011 at 16:29

It didn't even occur to me you could do art as a real job. So I never even looked.

Kathy Bloomingdale 17 September 2011 at 16:31 [Report]

Did you think people like Jason grew on a talent tree or something? So how did you find out about it? After you got home from confusing future beach-walkers with fake, bottled messages?

Madeline Cain 17 September 2011 at 16:33

No, I wasn't convinced you could actually do it as a thing. Claire had to drag me into a library and look it up before I'd believe her. This course even has a partial scholarship for overseas students.

Kathy Bloomingdale 17 September 2011 at 16:34 [Report]

I feel like this is too good to be true… About time one of us had some luck! So are you going for it?

Madeline Cain 17 September 2011 at 16:39

I don't know. They only take seven people per class, *seven*. All the blogs say it's the best course out there. I've only known about this for like, five minutes. What if I'm not any good?? Other people have probably been working on their application for a year. I could pin my hopes on this, not get in, and then be back to where I started. Is photography even a real job? I mean, everyone has a camera these days, why would you pay someone to do what you could do yourself? If it was easy to make a career wouldn't we have half a million photographers and our classes taught by robots? Because let's face it, who would voluntarily spend their time teaching pubescent boys who are probably imaging the teachers without their clothes?

Am I trying to build a bridge out of fairy-floss here to avoid making a real decision about my future? Unconsciously flipping-the-bird to my teachers because they can't *tell* me my perfect future career? What if I choose wrong and end up on welfare in a trailer park with trolls for children?

If you were me, what would you do?

Kathy Bloomingdale 17 September 2011 at 16:40 [Report]

Avoid reproducing with trolls for a start.

Madeline Cain 17 September 2011 at 16:41

Seriously!

Kathy Bloomingdale 17 September 2011 at 16:46 [Report]

If having trolls for children is a deep fear, then yes. As to the rest, unless you develop the Sight from being hit by lightning or some other space-time-continuum bullshit I'm sure Tim could elaborate on, you're going to just have to wing it like the rest of us.

For example, take my current predicament. If I'd known there'd be so many extra, boring things you needed to get to the good stuff, I may have never become a hermit for eight months to get here. But now I'm here it's suck-it-up-sunshine time. I thought it was going to be lots of design work and fittings and learning how to make extras look good without spending lots of money. You know, the important stuff. But there is sooooo much I didn't know I had to care about, like taking time to analyse films and write reports on the costumes, do historical research, or admit your mother was right and learn the actual art of dress making.

But the plus side is that even though I'm pretty sure my head will literally explode if I try to stuff anymore new information in, I'm actually more determined that all of this isn't going to come to nothing. I've gone through all this crap and it would be a waste if I didn't make it work. I was at the same knowledge level in costume design as you probably are in photography.

Madeline Cain 17 September 2011 at 16:47

You really think so? You're not just painting a turd gold here?

Kathy Bloomingdale 17 September 2011 at 16:50 [Report]

Now I have images of golden dancing turds in my head. It's lucky you're keen on photography and not journalism, your gift is *not* with beautiful metaphors.

Look, do a bit of research, play around with your fancy new camera. If it turns out you enjoy it even though you know it's going to be hard (and a less clear cut path than science), then maybe it's worth going out on a limb for it.

You said none of your school subjects actually excite you, so take the time to see if this does.

Madeline Cain 17 September 2011 at 16:51

Hmm, look who's creative *and* smart. If it could work for you maybe it will work for me.

Kathy Bloomingdale 17 September 2011 at 16:52 [Report]

If you give up turd metaphors anything is possible.

Madeline Cain Update #8, 365 Days of Fun: Photobomb as many people as you can. *Posted Sunday 18th September at 17:00* [Comment . Like]

> **Tim Gleeve** And selfie bomb. *Posted Sunday 18th September at 17:08* [Comment . Like]
>
> **Kathy Bloomingdale** What's that? *Posted Sunday 18th September at 17:10* [Comment . Like]
>
> **Tim Gleeve** When you offer to take a photo of someone on their phone, and between photos one and three you turn the camera around and take a selfie. A delightful surprise for future them. *Posted Sunday 18th September at 17:16* [Comment . Like]
>
> **Madeline Cain** Or a worrying sign of insanity for present them. When the person who holds their most precious possession looks like he's impersonating a bull dog or about to fart Skittles, well, you can imagine the results. *Posted Sunday 18th September at 17:20* [Comment . Like]
>
> **Kathy Bloomingdale** Photo three becoming a deer-in-the-headlight photo? *Posted Sunday 18th September at 17:21* [Comment . Like]
>
> **Madeline Cain** Bingo! *Posted Sunday 18th September at 17:24* [Comment . Like]
>
> **Tim Gleeve** Eternal memories of Mt Lofty will never be the same. *Posted Sunday 18th September at 17:26* [Comment . Like]

Wyate Yosime joined the group **Gordon Ramsey Rants.** [Like . Join]

> **Madeline Cain** What the *bleep?* I said a *little* spice not a *bleeping* fist full! Anyone who eats that'll be folding space and seeing the

bleeping future. *Posted Sunday 18th September at 18:38* [Comment . Like]

Tim Gleeve Just thought of the best way to dump a girlfriend: Interpretative dance! *Posted Sunday 18th September at 20:42* [Comment . Like]

> **Madeline Cain** You'd need a girlfriend first before you'd ever need to invent ways to dump her. *Posted Sunday 18th September at 20:49* [Comment . Like]

Madeline Cain Update #9: 365 Days of Fun: Walk up to a small child that resembles you and tell them you're from the future. *Posted Monday 19th September at 15:50* [Comment . Like]

> **Kathy Bloomingdale** That would've freaked me the hell out as a kid. *Posted Monday 19th September at 15:54* [Comment . Like]

> **Madeline Cain** Depends on how much the kid *doesn't* want to be like you. Tim got kicked in the shins by one. *Posted Monday 19th September at 15:55* [Comment . Like]

> **Tim Gleeve** At least I didn't make one cry. *Posted Monday 19th September at 15:56* [Comment . Like]

> **Madeline Cain** Claire was the most successful, mainly because her child was all business, "What are next week's lottery numbers? Can I avoid this whole height issue by eating green vegetables? Is Rex still alive? Am I famous? I'm not famous?! Where did you bugger up?" *Posted Monday 19th September at 15:59* [Comment . Like]

> **Kathy Bloomingdale** How old was this kid? She actually said 'bugger up'? *Posted Monday 19th September at 16:01* [Comment . Like]

> **Madeline Cain** Honest to God, from her mouth, to my ears, to

your eyes. *Posted Monday 19th September at 16:02* [Comment . Like]

Mike Cain joined the group **A Computer Can Beat Me At Chess, But It's No Match For Me At Kickboxing.** [Like . Join]

Madeline Cain Update #10, 365 Days of Fun: I thought going to the zoo was the fun for today. Turns out running out of the zoo shouting, "They're loose, run for your lives!" was the plan all along... *Posted Tuesday 20th September at 18:07* [Comment . Like]

Virginia Lowe The Earth is not dying, it's being killed! And the people killing it have names and addresses. It's time people stopped writing letters to their local politician and started taking emission trading schemes seriously. *Posted Tuesday 20th September at 21:12* [Comment . Like]

> **Tim Gleeve** Dear Iceberg, I heard about global warming. Isn't Karma a bitch? Sincerely, The Titanic. *Posted Tuesday 20th September at 21:53* [Comment . Like]

Madeline Cain Update #11, 365 Days of Fun: There is something so delightful about going into McDonalds and asking for a Happy Meal with extra Happy. *Posted Wednesday 21st September at 16:30* [Comment . Like]

Your Mission, If You Choose To Accept It... 365 Days Of Fun

NOTES > My Notes [Write a note]

By **Madeline Cain**. Thursday, 22 September 2011 at 19:09.

Claire and I have just done something my Mother has warned me never to do since before I can remember the internet being a thing. Now I can see why she was so concerned. I fear we may have stumbled on a cult.

Not one of those scary ones where you change your name and shave all the hair from your body before beating each other with rolls of salami for imagined sins, but one that none-the-less has very devoted followers with an unquestioning need to do whatever their leader asks. Even if that leader (verified or not) is asking very weird things of them.

What did we do to uncover such an organisation? Why would our method strike fear into my Mother's heart? Well, we took a phone number written on the wall of a public phone booth and used Claire's mobile phone to call it.

Yes, that's correct, we called the number of a stranger on a personal phone.

Cue ominous background music!

But rather than turning into Mum's worst imagined stranger-danger scenario, it became one of the most bizarre phone calls of my life. Because not only did we uncover a cult I never knew existed, we then high-jacked it from the original creator.

The nature of today's DoF had been a complete mystery, my only instruction being to kick around my house until Claire came for me. Little did I know my living room was to be the location for our unintentional cult high-jacking. Uncertain where we might be headed I had a winter jacket, several scarfs, swimmers, a towel and plastic poncho draped over the leather couch, and several pairs of boots scattered across the green and red Persian rug in readiness.

The doorbell rang after almost two hours of waiting and I skied in my socks along the wooden floorboards of our epically long hallway, almost colliding with the front door.

"Sup," Claire said, stepping inside and slipping out of a dripping rain coat. Her black hair was plastered to her head, giving the appearance of being painted on. "Where can we set up?"

"Here?" I unconsciously looked left and right for spying ears, even though I knew everyone else had left an hour earlier for some generic action flick showing at the cinema.

"I ain't going back out there." She jerked a thumb over her shoulder at the curtain of water.

As though accentuating her statement a gust of wind whipped straight through the door, rain drenching my front and making the floor even more precarious for klutzes like myself who are vertically challenged at the best of times.

I wrestled the door closed (without stacking it, win!) and after a quick debate with myself over freezing in the privacy of my room, or risk getting caught in the warmth, I opted for heating and led Claire into the living room.

Seeing the jumbled pile of clothing on the couch, Claire flopped to the floor, about as close to the heater as she could get without sitting on it. "Are you squatting in a display home or something?" She cast her eyes over the otherwise spotless room with its lounge suite, TV and half a dozen photo albums on a sideboard.

"Nope, Mum's got an obsession, it's like I'm already living in my mid-forties." I swept my arm across the leather couch, giving me enough room to sprawl. "So we're seriously not going anywhere. We're doing this... *thing* here?"

Claire slid her bag from her shoulder, flicking the catch open with a snap. "Sure are, I've got everything I need."

"And what exactly do we need? What are we even doing?"

"*This.*" With a flourish Claire placed a notepad, pen, her phone and a piece of paper with numbers scrawled across it on the rug in front of her. "We're going to call this number I found in a phone booth and see what happens."

"What!?" I slid from the couch, hissing as my knees smacked the floor. I snatched up the paper. Not only were there numbers on the paper, but the words 'Join Me' in spidery handwriting. "Why aren't we doing this at a phone booth? What if we lead lunatics in… in… pink tutus with samurai swords to my door??"

Claire snorted. "Unless we call a hacker, I doubt they'll be able to trace this number to our location. Let alone lead an army of samurai ballerinas to chop off our heads. I don't know if you've heard of this wonderful new setting they have on phones these days, it's called turning your number to private."

She made a 'give it here' motion with her fingers and I reluctantly handed her the paper.

"Fine. Your logic triumphs this time. What's the notepad and pen for then?"

"You'd make a poor detective. They're so we can discuss our next move without tipping off the person at the other end."

"Smart."

Claire winked, entering the number in the phone keypad at lightning speed and pressing send before I could utter another protest.

"Wait!" I hissed. "What are we going to say?"

Claire shuffled around to sit next to me. "What you normally say when you call someone."

"Hello?" chirped a high pitched voice.

I jumped and glared at Claire. She scribbled on the pad: *when in doubt, just repeat everything back to them.*

"Hello," replied Claire, wiggling her eyebrows at me. "How are you this fine day of torrential downpour?"

"Good?" The voice sounded young and was definitely female.

When Claire continued to cock her head expectantly, saying nothing, I grabbed a pen and scrawled, *Out of inspiration already?*

Patience ObiWan, was her sharp lettered response. She was right, we didn't have to wait long.

Voice sharp, the woman said, "Who is this? Why are you calling?"

Honesty? wrote Claire with a raised eyebrow. I crossed my arms and nodded. This was where I knew it would get weird.

"I found your number. On a wall," replied Claire.

The woman sucked in a hissing breath. "Oh my god! Oh my god! Is this really happening?"

Now it was Claire's turn for confusion, her cute little pixie face scrunching up at the nose. "Yes?"

"I know who you are!" The woman practically shouted.

My back stiffened and Claire and I shared a wide-eyed look.

"You know who we, I mean, *I* am??" repeated Claire.

It was like we'd opened a floodgate that we couldn't hope to stuff the conversation back into.

Barely leaving enough space between words to follow her, she said, "I thought I was supposed to find *your* number! But it's alright! It doesn't matter. I always say the world works in mysterious ways. Yes, yes I do! You throw your desires out into the world and they come to you! You found me! So… what do you want me to do?"

WTF?! I wrote.

"What do I want you to do?" Claire repeated back, almost automatically.

I shook my head. What a time to draw a blank.

"Yes, my mission! What's my mission, what do you want me to do?"

I tapped Claire on the shoulder and wrote, *Which missions have you heard about?*

Claire nodded and repeated the question out loud.

The woman didn't even pause to think. "There was that guy whose mission was to convince ten strangers on the street to give him something other than money. OH! And the guy you got to collect twenty different hats from people and then wear them all at the same time. And that time Timmy had to convince strangers at a restaurant to let him taste their food. Then there was the guy you got to refill Oreos with toothpaste and hand them out to the public as samples."

The sound of excited clapping burst from the speakers. "Oh, oh! There was that time you gave someone the mission of Newspapering their boss's room – that one was *epic!* There's nothing like covering every-single-thing in newspaper, even the stationary, am I right? Am I right? Then there was the guy who did Chinglish translations of all the Council signage in the CBD. Oh, of course, there was that time you got someone to Rickroll a stranger in real life by knocking on their door and singing *Never Gonna Give You Up* to their *face!* Classic."

What the hell is Rickrolling??? Claire wrote.

I shrugged.

"Hey," said the voice, "Hey... if you're the one calling *me,* does that mean you're going to give me a different kind of mission. You know, because you found my number and not the other way around?"

"Yes?" Claire hazarded.

"Oh thank god!" A sigh cracked in the speakers. "I was so worried that, you know, because it wasn't me who'd found *your* number in the phone booth, that I'd be penalised with some sort of shitty mission, like putting Kick Me signs on people's back or something. I'm *such* a big fan and I've been calling every phone number I've found for the last three months!"

See! Claire mouthed! I poked out my tongue.

"A big fan then," Claire said. "Maybe you can tell me your favourite mission and I'll tailor a more special mission for you."

"Can it be something like that one where you got people to cling wrap the car of someone who'd parked in a disabled zone when they weren't disabled? That was sweet. Not only is it hilarious but, you know, they like, also stood up for justice and stuff. You know, like a Karma Army or something."

"Hmmmm." Claire tapped a finger against her lips.

What are you thinking? I asked.

Claire gave a wolf-like grin, all wide mouthed and sharp teeth.

Claire... What are you thinking?!?! I ground my pen into the paper, almost tearing it.

"I've been saving this one for someone special," Claire declared.

"Yes! Yes I'll do it!"

I almost facepalmed. Seriously? Where did this girl come from? The school for the incredibly naive??

"I want you to go to your neighbours and borrow all of the ingredients you need to bake a cake."

"A-ha," said the woman. I could hear scratching noises, as though she were jotting things down with a pencil.

"You need to give each of these neighbours a thank you gift. In the form of dance. I want to see photos of some Macarenas or some Nutbush or-"

"The Hokey Pokey? I can totally do the Hokey Pokey!"

I pursed my lips together, the edges of the smile struggling to force it's way upwards. I could not laugh. *I could not laugh.*

Claire took one look at my face and had to turn her back. "Yep, that will do nicely. Then, I want you to give the cake that you make to a bake sale that's raising money for charity."

"Right, right," the woman muttered. "That's it?"

"That's it," replied Claire. "Do you think you can achieve this mission to my satisfaction?"

"I'm gonna be the best damn disciple ever! You just wait and see!" The line went silent for a moment and I thought we'd lost her. But no, oh no. "Um, look I know this isn't how you normally operate, but... can I pass your number onto some of my friends? They're even more hard core than me and it would mean the world to them. The world!"

I tapped Claire hard on the shoulder. *No!* I mouthed. *No!*

"Sure!"

I snatched at the phone but Claire jumped up, holding it out of my reach.

Claire rattled off some numbers and said, "But they've got to call me in the next hour. Otherwise they've missed their chance. This burner phone will be in the trash after 1pm."

"Roger!" replied the woman. "Over and out!"

I punched Claire hard in the arm as the phone screen flashed and went dark. "Are you insane!? You just high-jacked some crazy prankster cult!"

"Damn straight I did," she replied, rubbing her arm. "What a loser, getting people to do meaningless shit for his own amusement."

"And 365 Days of Fun is what?"

"Not sticking Kick Me signs to the back of someone's shirt," she shot back. "He's got all these people rushing around trying to find his number. To 'Join Him'. To be a part of something that's not only cool but has an impact. You heard her, she doesn't want some weird scavenger hunt, she wants to be part of a Karma Army. So that's what we're going to give them. Her and her friends. Every person who calls, we're going to get them doing awesome, random acts of kindness."

"Turn them from prankster to insane guardian angel," I mused, the possibilities leisurely teasing themselves out in my head.

"Exactly!"

The phone rang. Claire gave me a wicked grin. "It's for you."

So that's how we swiped a cult out from underneath a trickster's feet, unleashing a tide of wacky, left-of-field acts of kindness on Adelaide, who hadn't seen anything that bizarre since Fringe season.

I'll admit my first few suggestions weren't super creative. I instructed a couple to buy disposable cameras and take pictures of them making an old man happy, I had another buy a lottery ticket and leave it under the windscreen wiper of a random car, I convinced a footballer to put paid for book vouchers inside of popular books, and another to buy an old lady a hat etc etc.

But then they started getting more ambitious: give a policeman a helium balloon; place an ad in the local newspaper complimenting the reader on how awesome they were and oh, by the way, did they know a dragon would eat them if they didn't go out immediately and do something good for a stranger? Then there was setting up a free face-painting stall for kids in Rundle Mall, where every single child came out as equals, each and every one looking like a ninja turtle... no matter what animal they had requested going in.

By the end, ideas were being dredged from the bottom of the well. I convinced one guy to stuff a cardboard box full of party gear like feather bowers, hand-held fans, glitter and some serious eye makeup, which he was then instructed to take to the nearest gay-bar and distribute liberally.

And in my final call I got a girl to organise a night in honour of a recently sick acquaintance just out of cancer recovery. She will be printing his face on t-shirts, banners, paddle fans, cardboard masks, beer coasters, fake finger nails, bubble wands, superhero capes and any other merchandisable item she can get her hands (hello underwear!), to deck out the local pub for his surprise night. The best part was, she'd only met the guy once.

So sure, we could have gotten people to dump a million ping pong balls on Rundle Mall, we could have had people form a conga line that stopped traffic on Hindley Street, or had them herd sheep down the main street of Adelaide before 6am as is strangely allowed in the dated bylaws of this city. But instead we channelled the ridiculousness into acts of greater good, without anyone even blinking an eyelid.

Seriously, not one person questioned who we said we were. Not one of them told us we were getting too boring, or a little bit risk-ay. They took their orders with military precision and gushed about how amazing I (we, he?) was. Frankly, we could have had them give their clothes to a homeless man and streak down the street with nothing but body paint proclaiming 'Help the Homeless' to cover them, and they wouldn't have given it a second thought. That was the strength of our almighty power. Or the strength of their previous brainwashing.

Either way, now it's your turn. Not to streak, obviously, but to DO GOOD. Go on, go out there *right now!* Then come back here when you're done. This Facebook comment section will be waiting for you. Like a stalker in your shrubbery. Or a ninja turtle.

[Comment . Like . Share]

Adam Goldam and **10 others** like this.

Kathy Bloomingdale Wow, that was not how I expected this post to go down. It's like a fairy tale with clueless characters who trust too easily. You trust you won't get stalked by axe murderers with a perchance for ballet, and they in turn trust that you haven't just given them a mission that sees them in the slammer. This graffiti-driven trust worries me. As soon as that woman said, "I know who you are," I would have tapped out. It would be like my nightmares coming to life and pinching me on the bottom. *Posted Thursday 22nd September at 19:31* [Comment . Like]

> **Tim Gleeve** I'm a little disappointed your 'missions' didn't have more cross-dressing/costume store visits worked in. Or the sending of qualified masseuses to your friend's places of work for free massages *cough*cough* IT Direct *cough*cough*. *Posted Thursday 22nd September at 19:37* [Comment . Like]

> **Madeline Cain** Yeah, but we didn't want them doing the same stupid stuff the other person was making them do. Like sending them into the same room as you. *Posted Thursday 22nd September at 19:39* [Comment . Like]

> **Tim Gleeve** You mean the same kind of stuff you were doing when you call that number? *Posted Thursday 22nd September at 19:40* [Comment . Like]

> **Kathy Bloomingdale** Na-uh! I agree with Claire, 365 Days of Fun is *not* the same thing as what this guy was doing. He was getting people to be nuisances for his own amusement. You guys are trying to keep *yourselves* on the bright side of life. It's about you, not about grandstanding. For future reference though, if one of your 365 activities is to set up a cult, remind me never to join. I'm happy for you to hit people with salamis without me. *Posted Thursday 22nd September at 19:44* [Comment . Like]

Mike Cain What piss-weak missions! If I were Overlord of the Phone Booth cult, 'kick me' signs would be just the beginning! I'd instruct my subjects to go into the rooms of their siblings and duct tape anything not bolted down to the roof. I'd have them teach a stranger a break dance move they'd just invented. I'd have them fill their principle/boss/ parents/enemy's room to the roof with balloons! I'd have them lick things to claim them as their own! *Posted Thursday 22nd September at 19:56* [Comment . Like]

Tim Gleeve Build a fifteen person pyramid with pensioners! *Posted Thursday 22nd September at 19:58* [Comment . Like]

Mike Cain Go to the local Hindu temple and colour in all the shoe laces on the shoe racks with highlighter! *Posted Thursday 22nd September at 19:59* [Comment . Like]

Tim Gleeve Sit down and snap a selfie with an unknown family at every single restaurant in Gouger Street! *Posted Thursday 22nd September at 20:00* [Comment . Like]

Mike Cain Turn someone's sink/bathtub into an aquarium! *Posted Thursday 22nd September at 20:01* [Comment . Like]

Tim Gleeve Peg marshmallows at zoo animals! *Posted Thursday 22nd September at 20:02* [Comment . Like]

Mike Cain Too far dude. Too far. *Posted Thursday 22nd September at 20:03* [Comment . Like]

Madeline Cain How is it you'll condone stacking pensioners in a pyramid, or licking things to claim them, but you draw the line at marshmallows?? *Posted Thursday 22nd September at 20:05* [Comment . Like]

Mike Cain Animals can't brush their teeth, Madeline. What sort of monster are you? *Posted Thursday 22nd September at 20:06* [Comment . Like]

Derek Chan I know a guy who cling wrapped everything in another guy's bedroom, including the guy to his bed. I assume that guy was passed out at the time. *Posted Thursday 22nd September at 20:32* [Comment . Like]

Madeline Cain You'd hope so, because in all likelihood his scissors had just been cling wrapped to his desk. Wonder how he got his revenge? *Posted Thursday 22nd September at 20:36* [Comment . Like]

Derek Chan Remember, when in doubt, just *repeat everything back. ? Posted Thursday 22nd September at 20:38* [Comment . Like]

Ray Star Every time that sheep law comes up I just get the urge to be a very baaaaaaad boy *Posted Thursday 22nd September at 20:46* [Comment . Like]

> **Mike Cain** *Rolls eyes* Lame. *Posted Thursday 22nd September at 20:47* [Comment . Like]

> **Ray Star** Kids these days, they don't understand the art of a good pun. *Posted Thursday 22nd September at 20:49* [Comment . Like]

Katie Nikle Samurai ballerinas? Your brain must be a weird place to live. *Posted Thursday 22nd September at 20:51* [Comment . Like]

Tim Gleeve How can you not know what Rickrolling is?? *Posted Thursday 22nd September at 20:55* [Comment . Like]

> **Madeline Cain** Well then Mr I-can't-be-away-from-the-internet-or-i'll-die-from-lack-of-lol-catz, enlighten us. *Posted Thursday 22nd September at 20:58* [Comment . Like]

> **Tim Gleeve** It's only the most epic internet meme ever! A person, say someone like Mike, provides a hyperlink (you do know what one of those is, right?) to something seemingly relevant to the current topic, only to lead you to a music video of Rick Astley's 1987 hit 'Never Gonna Give You Up'. *Posted Thursday 22nd September at 21:04* [Comment . Like]

> **Madeline Cain** And a meme is? *Posted Thursday 22nd September at 21:06* [Comment . Like]

Tim Gleeve You…I…Ohmygod! *head explodes* *Posted Thursday 22nd September at 21:07* [Comment . Like]

Wyatee Yosime Toothpaste Oreos, om-nom-nom-gag! *Posted Thursday 22nd September at 21:20* [Comment . Like]

———

Tim Gleeve Madeline Cain You'll never believe what I found in the classifieds section! Or at least, my parents found. I feel like this is the same guy you convinced to put an ad of awesome in the newspaper involving dragons. Are you sure you worded your mission the way you thought you did?

> *"I'm sure most of you have seen the rather large green dragon that has been flying over the Salisbury area for the past week. I'm looking for someone to: a) lure said dragon to a more rural area; b) Force said dragon to land; c) Slay said dragon in whatever way you see fit. No pay, dragon slaying is its own reward. However I will tell you how 'awesome' 'brave' and 'good looking' you are in front of as big a crowd as you can amass. IMPORTANT NOTE: do not engage the red dragon that frequents the area. He and I have an understanding."*

Posted Friday 23rd September at 08:00 [Comment . Like]

Madeline Cain That is sooooooo, not what I told him to do! But that is the best ad I have ever seen. As Anchorman would say, "No, I'm not mad, I'm impressed!" *Posted Friday 23rd September at 08:07* [Comment . Like]

Kathy Bloomindale "Some disciples had deception in their hearts and betrayed their creator at the first task. And so it goes." *Posted Friday 23rd September at 08:10* [Comment . Like]

Madeline Cain A tale of caution and giggles... *Posted Friday 23rd September at 08:13* [Comment . Like]

Mike Cain "Your own notes should be cold. Merciless. Equal parts *Follow me if you want to live* and *Your clothes: give them to me now.*" My teacher is weird. *Posted Friday 23rd September at 13:13* [Comment . Like]

> **Tim Gleeve** Is this Mr Bolton? The one who gave me an English assignment with the instruction, "Write with these in mind and nothing will stop you. Except maybe a bear. Because bears are dicks." *Posted Friday 23rd September at 13:24* [Comment . Like]

> **Mike Cain** Yep, it's like you're in my nightmare... *Posted Friday 23rd September at 13:31* [Comment . Like]

Madeline Cain Update #13, 365 Days of Fun: Follow strangers around a store and spray everything they touch with disinfectant. *Posted Friday 23rd September at 16:20* [Comment . Like]

> **Kathy Bloomingdale** I assume the store's feedback emails are going to be *very* interesting for the next week. *Posted Friday 23rd September at 16:30* [Comment . Like]

> **Tim Gleeve** There's one complaint they can't make, the store will certainly be spotless... *Posted Friday 23rd September at 16:38* [Comment . Like]

Tim Gleeve I love this model of exercise so much right now I want to hug it like an anaconda. *Posted Friday 23rd September at 18:45* [Comment . Like]

> **Madeline Cain** You're playing Wii aren't you? *Posted Friday 23rd September at 18:53* [Comment . Like]

Tim Gleeve I'm playing Wii!!!! *Posted Friday 23rd September at 18:57* [Comment . Like]

Madeline Cain We need to teach you the difference between the real world and the matrix. *Posted Friday 23rd September at 18:59* [Comment . Like]

Kathy Bloomingdale likes the page **WHEN I READ CAPITALS, A VOICE IS SHOUTING IN MY HEAD.** [Like]

Kathy Bloomingdale So don't do it **Madeline Cain**. *Posted Friday 23rd September at 20:10* [Comment . Like]

Madeline Cain WHAT DID YOU SAY? I can't hear you on the other side of the world. *Posted Friday 23rd September at 20:24* [Comment . Like]

Madeline Cain Update #14, 365 Days of Fun: Greet a random person like a long lost friend and see if they play along. *Posted Saturday 24th September at 14:00* [Comment . Like]

Madeline Cain Adult victims are way more fun for this, kids and teenagers tell you immediately that they don't know who you are. But adults, even adults covered in full bodied tattoos, will play act until the cows come home rather than risk seeming like a dick. *Posted Saturday 24th September at 14:12* [Comment . Like]

Tim Gleeve *That's* why Claire was hi-fiving that grandma! *Posted Saturday 24th September at 14:16* [Comment . Like]

Kathy Bloomingdale Poor thing, she probably went home thinking she had the beginnings of dementia. *Posted Saturday 24th September at 14:18* [Comment . Like]

Kyle Traybna Oh 'Friends' how I love you:

Joey: That's how much our phone bill costs?!

Chandler: That's the phone number.

Posted Saturday 24th September at 15:02 [Comment . Like]

Wyate Yosime Errrrr excuse me, I bought a packet of chips, not half a bag of air! And while we're on the subject, McDonalds, wanna give me some coke with that ice? *Posted Saturday 24th September at 15:26* [Comment . Like]

Jack Fox Your birth certificate is an apology letter from the condom company ? *Posted Saturday 24th September at 15:47* [Comment . Like]

> **Tim Gleeve** Maybe *yours* is. Mine's a victory letter from Mother Nature. *Posted Saturday 24th September at 15:51* [Comment . Like]

> **Alex McMarshal** Couldn't ask for a better mistake baby ? *Posted Saturday 24th September at 15:55* [Comment . Like]

Kate Nikle likes the page **Dear Mr. Monopoly and Mr Pringles. Epic Moes Man.** [Like]

I'm Gonna Do It! [New Message]

[Back to messages. Mark as unread . Report spam . Delete]

Between **Kathy Bloomingdale, 2 others** and **You.**

Madeline Cain 24 September 2011 at 17:00

Alright, I'm gonna do it!! I'm throwing out the turd metaphors, I'm building a bridge of fairy floss and I'm going to commit to the seemingly impossible. Twelve months photography tutorage under my favourite artist of all time, in the greatest city of all time.

Kathy Bloomindale 24 September 2011 at 17:05 [Report]

Yay you! What finally made your decision?

Tim Gleeve 24 September 2011 at 17:06 [Report]

Turd metaphors?

Mike Cain 24 September 2011 at 17:08 [Report]

Turd metaphors? I've got plenty of those: I'm releasing the chocolate hostage; bombing Pearl Harbour; giving the lads a swim; I'm freeing some slaves; growing a tail…

Kathy Bloomindale 24 September 2011 at 17:09 [Report]

Why is Brother Mike here?

Madeline Cain 24 September 2011 at 17:10

Because even though he's, direct quote, 'An idiot', he can be creative in the wacky ideas department.

Mike Cain 24 September 2011 at 17:11 [Report]

Turd burgers, you don't hold back on the backhanded compliments do you, sis?

Madeline Cain 24 September 2011 at 17:11

Just keeping it real, bro.

Kathy Bloomingdale 24 September 2011 at 17:12 [Report]

Well this is going to be a lively conversation. So you made your decision...

Tim Gleeve 24 September 2011 at 17:12 [Report]

About... turd usage?

Madeline Cain 24 September 2011 at 17:15

Yes. No! Right, let me recap. I found out my favourite photographer runs a twelve-month course in New York every year. At first I wasn't sure if I should apply, the application is due in a couple of weeks and I've only ever done photography for fun.

So I decided to compare my potential creative and scientific career paths by hauling all of my National Geographic mags (from garage and library sales) out of the cupboard and going through them. I looked through all the amazeball pictures and found myself enthralled, excited, entertained and a thousand other descriptors starting with 'e'. Then I knuckled down and actually tried to read the scientific articles around the photographs. I almost flattened Adelaide with my earthquake level snores.

Mike Cain 24 September 2011 at 17:16 [Report]

Understandable. I get that every time a teach opens their mouth and says, "Open your textbook to page I-don't-care."

Kathy Bloomingdale 24 September 2011 at 17:18 [Report]

I never thought a magazine could be such an effective all-in-one decision maker. In saying that, I don't think you were the audience NG have in mind when they publish...

Madeline Cain 24 September 2011 at 17:18

Probably not, but it was a pretty effective eye-opener all the same.

Tim Gleeve 24 September 2011 at 17:19 [Report]

And you're telling us this because, what, you want a dysfunctional cheer squad?

Madeline Cain 24 September 2011 at 17:22

The point of this little online meeting is that I need brainstorming help. It's super competitive to get into the course, a new class opens every six months and only seven people get in each time. It means if I want to be chosen, I need a really clever portfolio piece. It has to tell a story, so it can't be half a dozen beach sunsets, or anything Jason specialises in (landscapes, wildlife and travel are his niches) because I don't have a hope of coming up to the standards of a pro. Not yet anyway.

Tim Gleeve 24 September 2011 at 17:25 [Report]

So you've cut out basically half the photographs you drool over in your magazine. Leaving us to come up with Andy Warhol type crap. Typical. When you told me to be home this afternoon I didn't realise I'd have to do thinking things.

Mike Cain 24 September 2011 at 17:28 [Report]

Save your brain Timmy boy, I've got this sorted. What we're going to do is break out the body paint. We'll paint ice-cream on chins, flies on foreheads, speakers on boobs, ducks on hands, snakes on... snakes. It's going to be a nude, yet not nude wonderland!

Tim Gleeve 24 September 2011 at 17:29 [Report]

Yes!

Madeline Cain 24 September 2011 at 17:29

No.

Kathy Bloomingdale 24 September 2011 at 17:29 [Report]

No.

Mike Cain 24 September 2011 at 17:30 [Report]

Alright, what about this? We do six portraits of serial killers dressed in, wait for it... actual cereal.

Madeline Cain 24 September 2011 at 17:31

Is this like the body paint thing but with cereal instead of body paint and a visit to jail instead of the park?

Mike Cain 24 September 2011 at 17:32 [Report]

Yes. Yes it is.

Madeline Cain 24 September 2011 at 17:32

Buzzzzzzzzz Yeah, no.

Kathy Bloomingdale 24 September 2011 at 17:35 [Report]

What about this, you could pick a *thing*. You know, like a colour, or an object and you go out and capture half a dozen awesome photos that focus on that theme. Imagine an album full of shoes!

Or you could do 'stills' from an unfinished movie. You know, something that suggests a huge cast and a much bigger story? Those could be in black and white, or sepia!

Or maybe you could have modern people, dressed in modern clothes, posing in the style of classic paintings.

Madeline Cain 24 September 2011 at 17:36

I'm not really a shoe person, but the movie thing could be fun…

Mike Cain 24 September 2011 at 17:38 [Report]

Sepia? Try septic. Are you trying to get Jason to flatten New York City with *his* snoring? No, that's all boring. What I think your submission needs is something sexy. Jason's a red-blooded male, appeal to his base needs. One of those needs is women in lingerie posing with things you find in the garden shed.

Tim Gleeve 24 September 2011 at 17:39 [Report]

How come when the Satisfaction girls do it, it's sexy, but when I wear a bikini and play with jackhammers I'm drunk and have to leave Bunnings?

Mike Cain 24 September 2011 at 17:40 [Report]

I know, it's a cruel, sexist, toolist world, my man.

Madeline Cain 24 September 2011 at 17:43

I was kind of thinking something along the lines of dressing up people in ye' olde clothes and putting them next to modern stuff, like a skyscraper, or a computer, or instant coffee. Or people in formalwear doing normal stuff like standing in line at the post office in a top hat and tails or picking up dog poo in an evening gown…

Kathy Bloomingdale 24 September 2011 at 17:45 [Report]

Oooh, I like the juxtaposition there. Maybe you could do one where the work uniforms don't match the activity like a ballerina in a tutu getting her hands greasy in a car engine, or a mechanic in his overalls dancing Swan Lake. That could be fun.

Just thinking on things I love seeing in the photos I buy, what about underwater photo shoots or something with mirrors?

Tim Gleeve 24 September 2011 at 17:46 [Report]

Or an underwater shoot WITH mirrors.

Kathy Bloomingdale 24 September 2011 at 17:47 [Report]

No need to be sarcastic. I don't see you contributing anything constructive.

Tim Gleeve 24 September 2011 at 17:48 [Report]

It's because I'm going to swing in like a knight in shining armour after all the lame ideas have been crushed.

Mike Cain 24 September 2011 at 17:50 [Report]

Let's super-charge those ideas, sis, from something lame to something deep and meaningful and... shit. If you want to take photos of actual people, you need to spice up the application with some cross-dressing portraits.

Kathy Bloomingdale 24 September 2011 at 17:51 [Report]

That's deep how?

Mike Cain 24 September 2011 at 17:51 [Report]

You know, examining gender stereotypes and other feminist agenda reasons you could bullshit about.

Tim Gleeve 24 September 2011 at 17:52 [Report]

Are you volunteering for that one, Mike?

Madeline Cain 24 September 2011 at 17:53

I think that's a little *too* political for this application, but I'm happy to help you fulfil your feminist agenda for one of your own assignments, bro.

Mike Cain 24 September 2011 at 17:54 [Report]

This is what I get for trying to be serious.

Madeline Cain 24 September 2011 at 17:55

Uhuh.

Tim Gleeve 24 September 2011 at 17:58 [Report]

I think after reaching this all-time low you will now appreciate my brilliant ideas. I'll even give you two options.

Option 1: People climbing ladders to nowhere. Super existential, meaning of life stuff there. Where are they going, what are they doing, do they have credit card machines up there or houses made of candy?

Option 2: Photos of people trying to squeeze into small spaces – boxes, bags, broom cupboards, Mike's brain. It's like the reverse clown car.

Madeline Cain 24 September 2011 at 17:59

Is it me or does this knight have a limp and no horse?

Kathy Bloomingdale 24 September 2011 at 18:00 [Report]

Indeed, he's all power and no finesse, like a monster truck.

Mike Cain 24 September 2011 at 18:03 [Report]

Fine, clearly I have to tame my inner creative tiger to get anywhere in this conversation. You don't want to take the risks that need taking? That's fine, you're scared, not everyone has a muse whispering sweet nothings in their ear. So here, this should get you over the line:

Mysterious portraits of people looking out the window, the only clue to what's going on outside is the expression on their face. Is it a parade of sausage dogs? A collapsing building? A zombie apocalypse? A flasher? Who knows!

Kathy Bloomingdale 24 September 2011 at 18:04 [Report]

That wasn't half-bad.

Mike Cain 24 September 2011 at 18:04 [Report]

Just coming down to your level.

Tim Gleeve 24 September 2011 at 18:05 [Report]

You'd take that over photos of large people forcing themselves into suitcases? Pfft. Where's the class I ask you?

Madeline Cain 24 September 2011 at 18:08

I really like that! But at the same time, they'd have to be close up photos which means you'd be able to tell they are fake emotions pretty quick. I don't want the photos to come off as overdramatic. But that *does* remind me of another project I saw where this guy took photos of a hundred strangers, just walked up to them on the street, and they weren't allowed to smile in the shot. And even though they weren't allowed to smile their face showed so much character!

Ooh! So what about this? Let's combine these ideas and go to the park to take photos of strangers when they aren't faking or suppressing their expressions. Like catching people having great big laughs?

Kathy Bloomingdale 24 September 2011 at 18:09 [Report]

Nice! Better yet, why don't you catch people in various shades of happiness and laughter? You could call that something like 'Shades of Joy'.

Madeline Cain 24 September 2011 at 18:10

I like it! It totally fits with my MO.

Tim Gleeve 24 September 2011 at 18:11 [Report]

What, you're killing people after you take their photograph? "Let me capture your beauty and then I will be the only one to see it ever after! Ha ha ha!"

Madeline Cain 24 September 2011 at 18:13

Eeew, no weirdo. You watch too many crime shows. What I mean is it matches my photographic ethos. In all the photos I take I'm trying to make the world a more happy and understanding place. Well, a more joyous place for *me*, but I'm sure I could extend it to an audience.

Mike Cain 24 September 2011 at 18:15 [Report]

Awwwwww, *gag*. Come on Mad, let's be real here, that's not adventurous enough. 'Be happy'? Please, if I wanted that I'd eat an inspirational book. Give me shock value any day. I can totally spice that idea up for you...

Madeline Cain 24 September 2011 at 18:16

No, absolutely not, you have served your purpose my village idiot. You inspired this idea and now I'm attached.

Mike Cain 24 September 2011 at 18:17 [Report]

Not on purpose! I was after sausage dog/flasher surprise, not people hugging each other and, God forbid, kissing.

Madeline Cain 24 September 2011 at 18:18

Ah, but your subconscious knew where this was going to end up. You're really good on the inside, even though you're a hardened evil genius on the outside.

Mike Cain 24 September 2011 at 18:19 [Report]

My subconscious was trying to get you to do something cool for once. Or get me on board this Days of Fun train you're riding...

Madeline Cain 24 September 2011 at 18:20

Nice try but no, you're going to have to be a million times less like yourself and a million times more like a Harry Potter house elf before I'd let you come on one of our missions.

Mike Cain 24 September 2011 at 18:21 [Report]

Then how the hell did Tim get welcomed with open arms?

Tim Gleeve 24 September 2011 at 18:22 [Report]

Hey now, don't drag me into this! I'm in because I bring the lols and don't wreck the joint.

Madeline Cain 24 September 2011 at 18:23

Tim is in because I need a Kathy substitute and he looks better in her clothes than you do.

Kathy Bloomingdale 24 September 2011 at 18:24 [Report]

Snort. Tim wishes he could looks as good as me in my polka dot dress.

Tim Gleeve 24 September 2011 at 18:25 [Report]

Pigs arse I'm the substitute! I bring the lols! And I have never, *ever,* tried on Kathy's clothes.

Mike Cain 24 September 2011 at 18:26 [Report]

So Maddie, are cross-dressing portraits more appealing with Tim as the subject?

Tim Gleeve 24 September 2011 at 18:27 [Report]

That's it, I'm tapping out. This is how rumours get started, people. You better be careful. It can just as easily go the other way...

Tim Gleeve left the conversation.

Mike Cain 24 September 2011 at 18:28 [Report]

That Days of Boredom thing was the only reason why I was humouring this little snore-fest. I'm out. Peace. Not.

Mike Cain left the conversation.

Kathy Bloomingdale 24 September 2011 at 18:28 [Report]

Boys are so weird.

Madeline Cain 24 September 2011 at 18:29

Yeah.

Mike Cain Rejection is just a challenge to go out there and do things better and with more style. If you can't join them, become a super-whopper-upsized copycat. *Posted Saturday 24th September at 19:00* [Comment . Like]

Tim Gleeve likes the page **Dear Buffy. We Have A New Assignment For You. His Name Is Edward.** [Like]

Kathy Bloomingdale Asked Dad why Mum was missing our Skype date. His reply: "She's off to see the witch and bring her a broomstick." *Posted Saturday 24th September at 19:06* [Comment . Like]

> **Madeline Cain** Visiting grandma? *Posted Saturday 24th September at 19:21* [Comment . Like]

Kathy Bloomingdale Visiting grandma. *Posted Saturday 24th September at 19:33* [Comment . Like]

Adam Goldbloom So I went for a job as a gym instructor and totally got it. It wasn't until I got there and was met with ten squealing girls that I realised the difference between gym instructor and gymnastics instructor is quite significant. *Posted Saturday 24th September at 19:50* [Comment . Like]

> **Tim Gleeve** Holy crappolla dude, did someone seriously give you a job teaching gymnastics?? How did you even get through the interview? *Posted Saturday 24th September at 19:53* [Comment . Like]

> **Adam Goldbloom** Flexed my guns and kept repeating, "Yep, I've got experience in that." *Posted Saturday 24th September at 19:57* [Comment . Like]

> **Madeline Cain** The old distract-them-with-your-guns trick. Gets the ladies every time. *Posted Saturday 24th September at 19:59* [Comment . Like]

Diana Lynal I should never be left alone in Kmart. *Posted Saturday 24th September at 20:30* [Comment . Like]

> **Kathy Bloomingdale** I have that exact same problem. *Posted Saturday 24th September at 20:50* [Comment . Like]

Lulu Tanaki Me: Toddlers like a smorgasboard of things to eat. Hubby: They also like wind on their face. *Posted Saturday 24th September at 21:16* [Comment . Like]

> **Madeline Cain** Kind of like a dog? *Posted Saturday 24th September at 21:20* [Comment . Like]

Kathy Bloomingdale How many shots were in that coffee yesterday?

I can SEE THROUGH TIME. *Posted Sunday 25th September at 06:56* [Comment . Like]

> **You** and **ten others** like this.

> **Madeline Cain** More all-nighters? *Posted Sunday 25th September at 08:45* [Comment . Like]

> **Kathy Bloomingdale** Yep. It's not as bad as it used to be though. I'm actually starting to *enjoy* all the random bits and pieces that go into being a costume designer. *Posted Sunday 25th September at 08:48* [Comment . Like]

> **Madeline Cain** So no more doubting it as a career? *Posted Sunday 25th September at 08:49* [Comment . Like]

> **Kathy Bloomingdale** I never said *that*. But the learning curve is getting less harsh. *Posted Sunday 25th September at 08:52* [Comment . Like]

> **Madeline Cain** That's all you can ask from life. *Posted Sunday 25th September at 08:54* [Comment . Like]

Kate Nikle likes the page **Zis Is Chaos. We Don't XXX Here.** [Like]

Madeline Cain This is the best idea we've ever had. We regret nothing. *Posted Sunday 25th September at 09:12* [Comment . Like]

> **Tim Gleeve** We apologise for nothing. *Posted Sunday 25th September at 09:13* [Comment . Like]

> **Madeline Cain** If anyone asks, we know nothing. *Posted Sunday 25th September at 09:14* [Comment . Like]

Very Mild Superpowers... 365 Days Of Fun

NOTES > My Notes [Write a note]

By **Madeline Cain** Sunday, 25 September 2011 at 13:30.

When you have a superpower (even a very mild superpower) it is a crime, a *crime* I tell you, to not use that power for good. But you have to do it properly. Which means you have to do it in costume. How else are you meant to be taken seriously?

So this morning, Literal Man, Fine Girl and I, Captain Spy Lens, donned our tights, our outside lycra underwear, our half masks, and our capes that flutter in the slightest of winds, and we took to the streets to fight petty crime and enforce justice!

This all started the day Claire introduced us to David O'Doherty's 'Very Mild Superpowers' song. As David crooned his out-of-tune mild superpower list (which included being frighteningly good at getting pens to work again and being able to successfully judge whether or not things will fit through doorways...) we worked on our own very mild superpowers.

Tim, was able to tell when people were interpreting rather than literally following rules; a mighty superpower. Claire could sense the appropriate punishment for any transgression, and I, I have the uncanny ability to catch people in the act of their very mild transgressions. We all had very mild superpowers, disused, languishing, and useless on their own. But joined together, in the League Against Petty Crime, we could be unstoppable!

We hatched our plan and arrived at the Haighs end of Rundle Mall at 9am sharp. I was the first there and was getting a host of subtle and not so subtle sideways looks. One guy almost ran into a pole in his effort to look but not look at me. I had gone ninja for my superhero suit, tightfitting black clothes top and bottom, a silver cape, underwear and mask, and my camera was covered in aluminium foil to match the design (lens free of foil, of course).

"Stealthy," drawled Claire, from behind.

I turned around and sniggered. "Where's your horse?"

While Claire had clearly tried for a police theme with her shiny blue and white square leggings and top, instead she'd come off looking like a race jockey.

She poked her tongue at me and pointed a finger towards Hindley Street. "At least I don't look like him."

A tram blocked our vision for a moment, the high pitch whine making me wince. Then the way cleared, the little green traffic-man allowed the crowd to cross the road, and I doubled over with laughter.

Tim was in a full body lycra suit, blue, which went from the tips of his toes to a hood that hooked over his forehead. Red underwear, mask, cape and a giant red L stitched to his chest completed the ensemble.

"You're loitering under a No Standing sign," declared Tim as he joined us. "That is a serious offense in Adelaide City, you should be ashamed of yourselves." He moved two meters back from the sign, out into the middle of the walkway and thumped fists to hips in what he probably thought was a dramatic pose.

I walked over and poked him hard in the stomach.

"Oof!" He doubled over.

"And you've jumped a Smurf and skinned them," I said.

"That's not on the list." Tim wheezed, slowly straightening.

"What, torturing a Smurf or poking you?"

"Both," said Claire. She fainted towards Tim's stomach with a cheeky grin and was rewarded with a flailing dodge from Tim.

Reaching into the waistband of her leggings, Claire pulled out a crumpled piece of paper and smoothed it out on her thigh. The page entitled, Petty Crime Scavenger Hunt, listed almost a dozen items from not wearing your bike helmet, to walking on grass where the sign says don't, to tackling people on skateboards in no skateboard areas, to being too loud in a quiet carriage, to not giving up your seat on a bus to an elderly person.

Tim edged towards us. "So do we do it in order?"

Claire looked up and shook her head. "Nope, as it comes. Starting with number seven. Jaywalker twelve o'clock!"

I spun around to face the intersection behind us, my cape flaring with a most satisfying snap. Then my camera was to my face, the shutter button down, and photos captured in a rat-a-tat-tat of sound. A young Asian woman hurried across the bitumen with her hands on the pink straps of her backpack and her silky hair fluttering behind her.

"Got 'em?" Claire cracked her neck to the right and left.

I checked the photos in play mode as the woman shuffled the last couple of steps to the sidewalk. "Ooh baby, do I ever!"

"Stop!" It was as though Tim had teleported from our side to suddenly reappear in front of our criminal.

I blinked. You think you know a guy then, *wham!* he becomes a superhero.

Claire nodded her approval. "He's got skills." Standing tall her expression collapsed into one of deadly seriousness and she strode towards the pair, whipping out a lined pad and pen from seemingly thin air.

"How many secret pockets do you have there? Have you got a unicorn up your sleeve too?" I asked, jogging after her.

My only response was a twitch in the corner of her mouth before it was game on.

Tim loomed over the woman, mouth set in a grim line. "You were jaywalking."

"Yeessss... I am walk." The woman looked at us, perplexed, eyes flicking from one 'hero' to the other in turn.

"No, you *jay*-walked," repeated Tim. "Walking with no green man. It's illegal. A crime against society. Against the world. Nay! Against the universe!"

Brows crinkled, the woman mouthed the words to herself.

Tim beckoned me forward. "Show her."

I displayed my evidence with a flourish, right hand gliding under the camera's view screen as though presenting a letter on the Price is Right. I flicked from one shot to the next pointing out the waiting crowd on the other side of the road, the red man, and her lone walk to the other side.

"Oh!" she nodded and smiled, her shoulders losing some of their tension. "Yes, a little… how you say… naughty. Yes?"

"Not naughty. Illegal. We'll have to fine you." Tim crossed his arms.

I almost felt sorry for the woman as her smile dropped and alarm set in. Then I steeled my heart against this hardened petty criminal. Superheros must stay strong!

"What's your name?" asked Claire, her tone brisk.

"Hu-long…"

"And where are you from?"

"Hong Kong but-"

Though we had agreed we'd stand there stony face after our part was done I couldn't help but stepped back to have a good view over Claire's shoulder. I realised in an instant why Claire had suggested it, I almost gave the game away as soon as I saw her pad. I spent a good minute choking on laughter as questions were rapped out by the others and answered haltingly by the woman.

Tim concluded the interrogation with, "Make sure this doesn't happen again. We know where you live."

Claire ripped the piece of paper she'd been working on off the pad, folded it in half and handed it over. "You can pay that at your local police station, post office or Italian eatery."

Then we split, leaving the woman to open her 'fine' and admire Claire's crazed portrait of Hu-long's head on the body of a tiny cat.

Things got more bizarre for our 'crims' from there. There were fines which required 50 apple pies to be delivered to their local old folks home for not smoking exactly two meters away from the doorway of a public building; fines which consisted of a grid of angry faces for the store clerk who took longer than the 'Back in five mins' sign indicated; and fines in which Claire had drawn a whole cartoon about how forest fires were started by stick people 'getting it on'.

A personal favourite was when we'd 'picked up' a particularly agro business man standing next to the No Standing sign. On that 'fine' Claire had written the following description:

Standing in a No Standing zone. Male. Probably a hundred years old. White? Would look like an Oompa Loompa with a green wig on. Appears to have had all the humour sucked out of him so his face looks like a dried lemon. He's given us some bullshit Cheery Tree Lane address, doesn't matter, after using my x-ray vision to look through his pants pocket I can see he works at Santos so can send the mob debt collectors there. As a consequence I also saw way too much of that mini-cocktail frankfurt he calls the family jewels. He should probably get that rash looked at.

Then there was the littering guy who'd dropped a McDonald's cup a meter short of the iconic bronze pig statues in the middle of Rundle Mall. He had to stand there as Claire ripped off page after page of 'incorrectly filled fines', and toss them, crumpled, at his feet.

"Gah! I keep getting my hero ID wrong!" she said, tossing yet another ball of paper to the ground. She then wrote the words '*don't be a punk*' on top of the new page, jotted down the number for Alcoholics Anonymous, drew a smile-y face, folded it in half and handed it to him.

"Finally. All done." She pointed at the scattered pages around his feet. "I'd pick those up and throw them away if I were you. They've got your name and number all over them."

All that went as well as could be expected. As the day wore on and Tim got more and more excitable, some people started to show their 'I'm not amused' faces. But most people seemed so dazzled by our costumes they could only manage a bemused expression and one word answers to our questions. We probably have shows like *Punked* and *Just for Laughs* to thank for that, no one wanted to be *that guy* who punched out an actor while on hidden camera.

But that was all before we staked out the 12 Items or Less line at the Woolworths supermarket and Tim got a little overzealous with Egg Man. You see, Egg Man had been having a bad day.

At the time I'd been busy scaring little children by wiggling my eyebrows at them when raised voices caught my attention. I turned to see Tim blocking the path of a man about two feet taller than him. Egg Man was probably a shift worker just doing some lunch time shopping in his high-vis shirt and workpants. But to Tim, this superhero we had let loose inch by inch, he was his biggest catch of the day.

"Why don't you want me to look in your bag sir? Do you have something to hide?" Tim pressed. He mirrored the man to the left and right as he tried to brush past.

"You're between me and sleep, bud." The man's voice was a low growl, the suitcases under his eyes echoed his claims for exhaustion.

"No, your poor decision to go through a 12 Items or Less aisle with more than twelve items is between you and sleep, *pal.*"

The man lifted his green shopping bag, shaking it in Tim's face. "The only items in here are muffins, bacon and eggs. Do the math ballerina."

"Yes, *a dozen* eggs if I'm not mistaken. Twelve eggs plus a pack of six muffins plus bacon is…" Tim pretended to count on his fingers. "Why that's a minimum of nineteen items, *more* once you reveal the number of bacon rashes you've tried to hide in that paper packaging."

Tim held up a finger and shook it. It was like a red flag to a bull. The man's face turned pink, and a vein on his forehead pulsed. Claire and I exchanged a glance and took one step back, then two.

To all this Tim seemed oblivious. "You have twice the allowable limit, sir. I'm afraid I'm going to have to put you under citizen's arrest."

To my amazement, Tim slipped his hand through a gap in the poor stitching around his L and whipped out a set of fluffy handcuffs. You could tell Tim had been itching to do this for hours, the look of glee on his face as he swung the cuffs from side to side was almost cartoonish.

"Next time you'll think twice about taking a dozen eggs through the express lane," he said.

"Where the heck did he get *those* from? Do you think he's got a portal to a sex shop in his hero suit?" whispered Claire.

I didn't realise how far away Claire and I had retreated until the manic look spread across Egg Man's face. There was no way we'd get to Tim in time to drag him away before shit went down.

The man loomed over him. "Think twice will I?"

He pulled out the egg carton, almost ripping the lid off as he flipped it back. I'm surprised he didn't crush the egg he pulled out, he was shaking so hard. "Think twice about *this* egg?"

I took one look at that face and thought, *yep, this is gonna happen.*

"Not. Likely," he said through gritted teeth.

His hand moved like a snake, giving Tim no time to react. The egg slammed down on the crown of his lycra covered head, yellow yoke and snot like membrane exploding out in all directions. Slime dripped down Tim's forehead and into his eye as he scrambled backward, slipping on goo.

"Here, have another! And another!" Egg Man was moving full steam by this point, pelting the yelping Tim with egg after egg to the applause of some teenagers at the check in counter.

"Eggs and stones may break my bones but vengeance will be mine!" cried Tim, before taking one right in the groin.

As Tim collapsed, groaning in a slick puddle of gunk, Egg Man held his hands up in fists of victory and tossed the empty egg carton onto Tim as he exited the store and was lost in the crowd.

Claire and I ventured forward, standing over him with hands on hips.

"Dude," said Claire, shaking her head.

"Sex-cuffs? Has planet Krypton given you no sense, Super Tim?" I added.

As we gazed down at him polished black boots joined our little circle.

"What the hell is this?" snapped a voice.

We looked up and stared at a balding security guard, glowering at us in turn. I'm not sure why we were so surprised, it had been pure luck that we hadn't been run out of the open air mall before then. Yet nowhere in our discussions had we even thought to create a false story we'd tell security if they decided superheros in the mall was bad for business.

"No? Nothing? Mime got your tongue?" he asked.

Silence.

The guard pursed his lips. "Right. If that's the way it's going to be, it's time I got the police involved."

"No!" I came up short, silently cursing myself for being the one to break first. Why couldn't Tim have gotten himself out of his own mess? Literally.

"What's your name?"

"Madeline Cain," I replied without thinking, then cursed myself again. We *had* code names, why didn't I have the sense to use Captain Spy Lens?

It was time to take charge of the situation. I took a deep breath and hoped Tim would keep his mouth shut for once. "I'm so sorry we didn't get to him in time, sir. My aunt would be so angry if she knew we'd taken him out without permission."

The guard frowned. "What?"

"My cousin," I said, pointing to the suddenly still Tim. "He's... special. We're only supposed to take him on outings when there's a carer about, but he overheard us talking about dressing up this weekend, and we just.... We just couldn't tell him he wasn't able to come. We thought we could handle him but..."

Thrusting a stubby finger at Tim the guard said, "Are you say he's retar- I mean, he mentally disabled?"

I gave him the severest look I could muster. "We don't use the term 'disabled' any more, sir. It's negative."

He crossed his arms and lifted an eyebrow as if to say, *ahuh, I'm this close to lighting your pants on fire, liar.*

It seemed desperate pleading was our best, last chance... "Please sir. We'll grab a mop and we'll clean this mess up. My aunt was *this close* to letting me take him on outings on my own. Don't let my screw-up place him under house arrest again. We'll clean everything up and no-one needs to know."

"Don't wanna go home," Tim mumbled at our feet. For emphasis he slapped his hand against a particularly slimy patch of egg.

Clarie wrinkled her nose and lent down to pat Tim on the shoulder (but really, we all knew she was just trying to brush egg off her lycra pants with her other hand). "Shhhh, little plonker," she said in her thickest Irish accent. She looked up through her fringe to bat her eyelids at the guard.

The man sighed and rolled his eyes. "You *will* clean this mess up. And then I don't want to see you around here for the rest of the day. Kapeesh?"

We nodded.

And that, ladies and gentlemen is how you get out of being detained by security guards. In a world where your friend is a (fake?) retard, and you're wearing lycra, you can get away with anything...

[Comment . Like . Share]

Adam Goldam and **10 others** like this.

Tim Gleeve Didn't think that one through, did I Space Tim? *Posted Sunday 25th September at 13:40* [Comment . Like]

>   **Kathy Bloomingdale** No, you didn't. Space Tim? *Posted Sunday 25th September at 13:44* [Comment . Like]
>
>   **Tim Gleeve** Literal Man was just a cover ID. My true identity is Space Tim from Planet Awesome. *Posted Sunday 25th September at 13:45* [Comment . Like]
>
>   **Madeline Cain** Then again, did you think through any of our encounters before you opened your mouth? *Posted Sunday 25th September at 13:46* [Comment . Like]
>
>   **Tim Gleeve** I choose to ignore that comment and instead take extreme offense to the question mark you put after 'fake'. *Posted Sunday 25th September at 13:47* [Comment . Like]
>
>   **Madeline Cain** You do that plonker. *Posted Sunday 25th September at 13:47* [Comment . Like]
>
>   **Tim Gleeve** Seriously! That does that even mean?! *Posted Sunday 25th September at 13:47* [Comment . Like]
>
>   **Kathy Bloomingdale** Idiot. *Posted Sunday 25th September at 13:48* [Comment . Like]
>
>   **Tim Gleeve** Not knowing what it means doesn't make me an idiot. It makes me normal. *Posted Sunday 25th September at 13:48* [Comment . Like]

Kathy Bloomingdale No you idiot, in Ireland it means 'idiot'. *Posted Sunday 25th September at 13:49* [Comment . Like]

Jack Fox My very mild superpower is knowing when someone needs loving, and I'm happy to provide ? *Posted Sunday 25th September at 13:55* [Comment . Like]

Alexa McMarshall And my superpower is accepting love. Look, we match! *Posted Sunday 25th September at 13:58* [Comment . Like]

Tim Gleeve Gag! I'd ask you two to suppress your superpowers around me otherwise we're going to end up in a very awkward threesome. *Posted Sunday 25th September at 13:59* [Comment . Like]

Diana Lynal Mine is knowing when someone is a lying, cheating, a-hole! *Posted Sunday 25th September at 14:00* [Comment . Like]

Madeline Cain Wow, D, something happen? Wanna talk about it? *Posted Sunday 25th September at 14:01* [Comment . Like]

Diana Lynal No more talking, only revenge. *Posted Sunday 25th September at 14:01* [Comment . Like]

Madeline Cain Ok then. *Posted Sunday 25th September at 14:02* [Comment . Like]

Kathy Bloomingdale I *must* see those photos, particularly if you've any of Tim being pelted by eggs. He never did have any sense, that's why he spends so much time on the internet. Most people don't have any sense there. If it was me, I'd have put him in a full-faced lycra suit. A green one. You could've called him Gumbie Man. *Posted Sunday 25th September at 14:10* [Comment . Like]

Madeline Cain My finger may have pressed the shutter button once or twice during the incident... *Posted Sunday 25th September at 14:13* [Comment . Like]

Tim Gleeve I knew it! You two never meant to help me! You brought me along as bait for your photography experiments! *Posted Sunday 25th September at 14:14* [Comment . Like]

Kathy Bloomingdale Sounds to me like you brought yourself along as bait buddy. *Posted Sunday 25th September at 14:15* [Comment . Like]

Tim Gleeve You weren't in the trenches. You don't know what it was like, man. The power, the glory. It changes you. *Posted Sunday 25th September at 14:16* [Comment . Like]

Kathy Bloomingdale What was going through your head when you decided to antagonise a man double your size? *Posted Sunday 25th September at 14:17* [Comment . Like]

Tim Gleeve He has a dozen eggs, now I can put my glorious plan into action? *Posted Sunday 25th September at 14:17* [Comment . Like]

Kathy Bloomingdale And when you taunted him to the point of throwing an egg at your nuts? *Posted Sunday 25th September at 14:18* [Comment . Like]

Tim Gleeve I was going for the classic superhero-movie half-way point, a vow of revenge. *Posted Sunday 25th September at 14:19* [Comment . Like]

Madeline Cain As I thought, nothing but lucky charms in there. *Posted Sunday 25th September at 14:19* [Comment . Like]

Kathy Bloomingdale Next time you hatch a Day of Fun scheme, try not to almost get yourself arrested, ok? *Posted Sunday 25th September at 14:20* [Comment . Like]

Madeline Cain Ah yes, but I wasn't the one covered in raw egg. I'm not stupid enough to do anything that would *actually* get me caught. *Posted Sunday 25th September at 14:21* [Comment . Like]

Tim Gleeve When you're above the law, nothing can stop you! *Posted Sunday 25th September at 14:22* [Comment . Like]

Kathy Bloomingdale Uhuh. I just realised, where the heck is Mike? I thought he'd be having a field day with this. *Posted Sunday 25th September at 14:23* [Comment . Like]

Madeline Cain Beats me. I don't keep tabs on him. That's Mum's job. *Posted Sunday 25th September at 14:24* [Comment . Like]

Derek Chan You guys should've totally come to me for weird punishment ideas, my parents are the masters! Once, in primary school, they made me wear one of those cones you put around dog's heads to stop them licking their balls. *Posted Sunday 25th September at 14:30* [Comment . Like]

Madeline Cain That was in punishment of... *Posted Sunday 25th September at 14:33* [Comment . Like]

Derek Chan I was biting other kids. It only took about five minutes in the cone to decide I was never going to pretend to be a vampire again. *Posted Sunday 25th September at 14:35* [Comment . Like]

Mike Cain likes the page **Waving To The Security Cameras When You Enter A Store.** [Like]

Kate Nikles likes the page **You're Never Too Old To Say Something Inappropriate.** [Like]

Kathy Bloomingdale I laughed so hard at this sign today, the janitor must be bored: Escalator acting like stairs. *Posted Sunday 25th September at 14:38* [Comment . Like]

> **You** and **5 other people** like this.

Madeline Cain I just got the weirdest text from Mum, "You better be home before 6pm, or we're going to have some serious words." It can't be that bad if she's giving me three hours to get home, right? *Posted Sunday 25th September at 14:40* [Comment . Like]

> **Tim Gleeve** I wouldn't be so sure. I think I know what that's about. You better PM me. And while you're at it, I'd poke your brother too. *Posted Sunday 25th September at 14:46* [Comment . Like]
>
> **Madeline Cain** Mike? What's Mike got to do with this? *Posted Sunday 25th September at 14:48* [Comment . Like]
>
> **Tim Gleeve** Seriously. PM me. *Posted Sunday 25th September at 14:50* [Comment . Like]

Mike Cain What is it with mothers? They get their panties all whirled around in some kinda panty tornado. *Posted Sunday 25th September at 14:55* [Comment . Like]

PM Me

Tim Gleeve

Today   [Clear Chat history]

I think I know why your mum is sending you threatening text messages.

So it *was* a threat?

Pretty sure she's going to have some 'serious words' with you whether or not you get home by 6pm. So I'd just not go home.

What the hell is going on here? Tell me what you know Space Tim!

Your brother was in the supermarket. Following people.

Ok, so that's weird but at the same time *how are you still in Rundle Mall without being jailed!?*

I was watching from behind a giant newspaper. With binoculars. The Advertiser is great for camouflage.

Tim, you were in spandex. I don't think the newspaper would have helped.

The old lady next to me said I had nice legs ;)

Snort. And what did she say about the binoculars? Where the hell did you even store those?? How did you and Claire manage to make yourselves bloody ninja suits??

Mike Cain

Today   [Clear Chat history]

Mike, why is mum sending me ominous texts? This has a fishy smell of something *you* would instigate.

Hey, you started it.

Started what? What did you tell her?

The truth.

Don't be a little shit. The 'truth' has a whole book series worth of shades of grey with you. What kind of truth?

The truth that you were the reason I was doing what I was doing when I got caught by security.

What are you blaming me for now!?

Giving me ideas.

I apparently gave you the idea of following people around a supermarket? You sure you didn't get that one from like, society in general?

Who told you that?

Tim.

Gah! Foiled by a lycra wearing Power Ranger!

Ha! I told Tim the newspaper wouldn't hide him.

That's not important, what's important is what I saw *through* those binoculars. And that's Mike, following middle aged ladies around a supermarket, drinking out of a Windex bottle.

I didn't see him. I was reading your FB note when you started bugging me about parental texts.

YOU WERE DRINKING OUT OF A WINDEX BOTTLE?!

What?!

Maybe.

If he's not in a hospital by now I'd say he replaced the Windex with something not likely to have him spasm like a possessed child from the Exorcist.

Are you in hospital?

:D Nope. It was totally Gatorade.

Why would you do that?

What is even the purpose of that??

As far as I can tell, he was doing it so that people would freak out and tell the woman he was following that her 'son' was drinking window cleaner. The woman freaks out, turns and sees Mike who is definitely not her son. Mike gives a Cheshire-Cat grin and runs off.

Because if I didn't I would have massive stomach cramps and an intense case of poisoning. Duh.

You *know* that's not what I meant.

Because somebody is a huge scrooge and wouldn't let me join in her games.

So he's messing with them?

Parodying you is my guess. This has 365 Days of Fun written all over it.

So you what? You start your own warped version of DoF by pretending to poison yourself?

Damn it! This is all Facebook's fault, if we hadn't 'friended' Mike, he would've been none the wiser. I actively avoid him in real life. He would've had about as much knowledge as the 'rents.

Start? Pffft, young Jedi, I've been at this for at least a week.

I'm sorry, I think there was a glitch in the Matrix because I could've sworn you just confessed to multiple accounts of terrorising the location population.

Just tell your Mum he's taken an innocent idea and warped it so you can't tell which way the arse is facing.

If you call putting letters into people's letter boxes telling them I know where they live, as 'terrorising the location population' then call me guilty! I confess.

Sadly, the fact that I didn't actively *discourage* him is enough to induce a lecture.

Yes! That is 305% classified as terrorising the local population!

But you didn't know.

Doesn't mean a bucket of llama spit when it comes to my Mum.

Ah. You have an unreasonable parent then. I'm sorry but I cannot help you.

Apparently he's been at it for a week! Which means as soon as neighbours start complaining about the weird thing that happened to them this week Mum is going to join the dots and I'll be in even *more* trouble.

It's like Ground Hog Day but with you getting framed for your brother's genius over and over.

I think you mean 'evil'. Holy sand dragons, the security guard who picked up Mike remembered my name! Now I'll get the blame for both of your stupidities!

Hey, I wasn't the one who gave him my real name. Watch which stereotypes you're flinging about.

Facepalm Which has now resulted in Mum joining together some completely unreasonable dots. I better get home before she gets the chance to distil her rage any further.

I'd say you have a sunny chance of ass-kicking there. Good luck Captain.

Filling me with optimism as always Super Tim.

They should be thanking me. I've made this the safest street in town. They now have the 'evidence' they need to get the police acting as a free security service.

Oh my god does Mum know about that one too??

Shrug, who can tell, she's in one of her 'I'm not speaking to you' rages at the moment. I think it's because when I told her I was just doing what you were doing, the security guard asked if I was related to you and your retard cousin.

Oh no no no no!

Am I going to find out about this if I read the rest of your note? Because from what I understand, a good egging was involved. I'm proud of you, sis.

If you read the note you'd know it wasn't me.

Sigh, I *knew* you weren't cool enough to pull that off. What can a brother do but make up for your lack of coolness?

Certainly not bring his sister in to deflect his mother's wrath!

We both know I tagged you into the ring because you're a genius at getting Mum to come down off her high horse.

Yeah but she's never *texted* me a warning before.

Come on, it was just some practical jokes. How much worse can it be than the last time we got into trouble?

Shit Hit The Fan [New Message]

[Back to messages. Mark as unread . Report spam . Delete]

Between **Kathy Bloomingdale** and **You.**

Madeline Cain 26 September 2011 at 10:00

This is sooooo much worse than the last time I got in trouble! And my expectations were low to begin with. I feel like I've been hit by a firework propelled freight train.

Kathy Bloomindale 26 September 2011 at 10:10 [Report]

What's so much worse than last time? Are you ok? Did you try jumping off the Glenelg jetty again? I keep telling you, you shouldn't leap with starfish arms. You get a wedgy every time.

Madeline Cain 26 September 2011 at 10:13

French the Llama! I keep forgetting who I've been having my conversations with on this damn website. This afternoon I got a very threatening text from Mum telling me to be home. After consulting Tim and my weasel of a brother Michael I determined that Mike had been imitating 365 Days of Fun in his own supervillain way, had been caught by security, and then offered me up as a sacrifice to our Mother.

Kathy Bloomingdale 26 September 2011 at 10:15 [Report]

This makes me so glad I only have a sister, the classic 'she did it first' ploy is always of the milder variety. But come on, your Mum knows Mike and she knows you, she'd know Mike was taking things to the extreme. Unless... Oh no!

Madeline Cain 26 September 2011 at 10:16

Oh yes.

Kathy Bloomingdale 26 September 2011 at 10:17 [Report]

Unless that was the security guard you stupidly gave your name to today hence suddenly putting you on the same playing field as your brother! Well, in her eyes at least.

Madeline Cain 26 September 2011 at 10:18

Hey! Can we ease up on the name calling right now? Hit by a freight train remember?

Kathy Bloomingdale 26 September 2011 at 10:19 [Report]

Sorry! But man, that's some bad luck. What God did you screw over recently?

Madeline Cain 26 September 2011 at 10:21

It must've been multiple ones because the security guard wasn't the only one who had words with my Mother about me. Miss Kennedy bailed Mum up while she was food shopping this morning. Apparently she'd a story to relay about my performance in a certain interview…

Kathy Bloomingdale 26 September 2011 at 10:21 [Report]

Oh god, and your Mum joined some dots?

Madeline Cain 26 September 2011 at 10:21

Yep, she's good at that.

Kathy Bloomingdale 26 September 2011 at 10:22 [Report]

Your Mum could out squiggle Mr Squiggle any day.

Madeline Cain 26 September 2011 at 10:32

It wouldn't even be a competition. She's so 'good' at seeing patterns that she once narrated an entire play to me from shapes she'd found in the clouds. Once she thinks she's found a pattern, she never lets it go.

The lecture, and yes, it was a lecture, an entirely one way exchange that involved being talked *at* rather than *to,* was in the living room (as always). The first words out of her mouth were so completely unexpected that I was thrown for the rest of the time and couldn't even summon up my pre-prepared defence.

I was sitting on the edge of the couch and she was pacing the rug, her arms crossed. When she's pacing it's always a bad sign. It meant she was in her drill sergeant mode, an automatic armour from her Army reserve days.

"Miss Kennedy has informed me of some interesting developments in your attitude over the past several weeks." The surprise on my face caused only the barest hesitation before she barrelled on. "She tells me her colleague on the university board was very disappointed at the farce you made of the early entry interview. Particularly when you'd come with such high recommendations."

"I-" What would have come out of my mouth then was anybody guess. *I poop planets*, probably, I was that thrown off course.

Mum held up a finger. "No. I'm sure the excuses will come thick and fast but you *will* listen to me first. You *threw* a highly important interview, Madeline! One that was instrumental to the next decade of your life! Miss Kennedy has been watching you ever since. She says you've started handing your assignments in at the last minute, not paying any attention to classes or the notes teachers have been giving you about the extra extension sessions you've *missed* even though you made a *commitment* to attend them at the start of the term. She is *very* concerned you're not taking your future seriously. Now I know why."

I craned my neck up as she stood directly in front of me, glaring down.

"You were playing *games.*"

Kathy Bloomingdale 26 September 2011 at 10:33 [Report]

Maddie, you were skipping extension classes?

Madeline Cain 26 September 2011 at 10:35

I needed some space! That was seriously all you got from that? She called 365 Days of Fun a game, like I was Mike just playing at life, poking a bear to see if it tried to eat me. I'm nothing like Mike! I was *not* poking a bear, and 365 DoF had nothing to do with why I threw the interview in the first place, it's a totally unfair assumption that the two are connected!

Kathy Bloomingdale 26 September 2011 at 10:37 [Report]

Sure, but you need to at least tell the teachers you're withdrawing, you can't just ignore them for weeks. Sorry, I didn't mean that to be the first thing I typed, but you can't deny that makes things look extra bad. Did you get to tell her why you threw the interview?

Madeline Cain 26 September 2011 at 10:43

They were volunteer sessions, I didn't think it would matter if I didn't show up! Yet another thing that I thought was tiny in the grand scheme of things and has been suddenly made a cornerstone in my Mother's pattern.

And no, I didn't get any chance to explain to her why I didn't do well in the interview. In fact I basically got as far as, "My grades aren't affected–" before she came down on me like a sack of hippos.

"Not yet! But if you keep this up you'll do more than affect your grades, you'll affect your future! Almost getting arrested by the police, being a public nuisance, all of that can go on your record. I've never had to have *this* talk with you and now I'm wondering…I need you to tell me right now, truthfully, are you on drugs?"

I looked at her like she'd grown two llama heads and started doing the CanCan. "Mum! Eew no!"

Kathy Bloomingdale 26 September 2011 at 10:44 [Report]

She seriously asked you if you were on drugs?? You, who holds your breath around smokers and coughs like a crazy person if you get a whiff of woodfire smoke in your nostrils?

Madeline Cain 26 September 2011 at 10:59

I know right!

Then she says, "I know you've been working hard a long time and it seems like you'll never have fun again, but it's less than two months. Less than two months to actually give yourself a solid start or screw up your future prospects. Games are fun but they're not *real* Madeline. Like art, like theatre, like street performing, like dog walking, it should be a hobby, not a ruling part, these things can't make you money you can live off. If they could all of us would just play games and have fun and life would be puppies and rainbows! But it's not, ok? At the very least if you don't want a lifetime career out of your University degree it will give you a back-up plan! Something you can rely on to make money and be able to live. Without money, without a degree, what are you qualified for? Nothing but baseline jobs, check out chicks and hospitality workers who earn half of what Daddy and I earn and we're *not* rich."

Seeing as my carefully prepared irrefutably logical defence of blaming the crap out of my brother was not fitting this scenario I threw it out the window and tried to free-ball it. Always a bad idea when you're facing a drill sergeant who has been stoking her anger for hours. "Mum, none of this is related to each other. The stuff I've been doing outside of school has nothing to do with my future. I have a plan! Just because it doesn't match Miss Kennedy's high and mighty-"

"Enough!" Mum snapped and I jerked back. That was when I realised I was not within one of our regular discussions.

"This is no time to be dramatic." Her foot stamped out a staccato rhythm you could time by. "You need to knuckle down and work. I refuse to be one of those parents who sees her child in crisis and doesn't have enough balls to be strict when they need it most. I will not repeat the same mistakes my parents made. I will not see my daughter lose her ambition and float without a place in the world."

"I'm not-"

She held up a hand again and I fell into automatic silence. "No. I'm willing to have you hate me for the next month. I'll be the bad guy if that's what it takes. You're grounded for the next two weeks. The only time you will leave this house is in the company of your father or myself. You will make up for all the study you've missed 'playing around' and you will have *plenty* of free time to contemplate what you're going to do with your life."

Kathy Bloomingdale 26 September 2011 at 11:00 [Report]

But the next two weeks is school holidays!! You need to get your application together for Jason's course!

Madeline Cain 26 September 2011 at 11:05

I know, I know! The only reason I hadn't completely collapsed at school was because I knew the holidays were coming, and that as scary as it was, I could finally find out if someone else thought I could do this photography thing. Now, it looks like I don't get *any* of that unless I sneak out of the house! So I have to engage in *more* behaviour that makes my mother think I'm doing drugs. And there's no way I can talk her around to giving me one day to do my photos, you heard what she thinks of an arts career!

The worst part is, when I was sent to my room I started doubting everything I'd been planning. It's always in the back of my mind that thousands of people do art courses across the world and only a handful actually get to put what they know into practise and make money off of it.

Kathy Bloomingdale 26 September 2011 at 11:07 [Report]

Look, you may say I've a bad case of the optimism virus, but I think you're one of those people who'd make it work. An arts career I mean, not necessarily sneaking out of the house. You and sneaking have historically always ended on bad terms. I'd get outside, Irish-born help for that one.

Madeline Cain 26 September 2011 at 11:08

If only that were a real virus. And if only I hadn't been on a roll yesterday and flambéed my friendship with Claire.

Kathy Bloomingdale 26 September 2011 at 11:09 [Report]

I'm not following.

Madeline Cain 26 September 2011 at 11:10

I set fire to the friendship ok?! I didn't do it on purpose.

Kathy Bloomingdale 26 September 2011 at 11:10 [Report]

Obviously. What happened?

Madeline Cain 26 September 2011 at 11:14

I was hanging out with Claire when I found out Mum was creating her inner Hulk for our afternoon 'meeting'. So later on that evening she did what she always does, and didn't check the emergency stay-away texts I sent her (because she doesn't 'do' technology) and just turned up at the front door asking for me.

So Mum tells her to go away, stalks up to my room and confiscates my phone because I'm supposed to be 'working' not 'texting'. Which just fuelled the inner ball of confusion and anger and hurt. It was in this state that Claire tapped on my window demanding to be let in.

Kathy Bloomingdale 26 September 2011 at 11:15 [Report]

Wait, what? Your bedroom is in the second story!

Madeline Cain 26 September 2011 at 11:25

She'd snuck around the back and climbed from the bins to the shed to the veranda roof to my bedroom window. I struggled to open the stiff window as quietly as possible and let her roll her way over the sill and onto my carpet.

She jumped to her feet. "Ta-da!"

I glared at her. "Claire? What the hell? Why didn't you listen to my messages?"

"You know I don't check that thing." She waved a hand lazily.

"Yeah, well not only am I now grounded for two weeks but you showing up at the door had Mum confiscate my phone."

Looking at her feet she said, "Sorry about that. I just wanted to see if you were ok."

"Well clearly I'm not. I have to study! And make decisions! And pick some sort of back up career so I don't live a life of eternal poverty!"

If you'd been there you'd have recognised that as a sarcastic impression of my Mother, but Claire hasn't known me as long as you have…

Kathy Bloomingdale 26 September 2011 at 11:26 [Report]

So she thought you were serious.

Madeline Cain 26 September 2011 at 11:28

Not only serious, but that I'd regressed to the state I was in when I first met her.

"Is that what your mother thinks?" she asked.

"Of course she does! And she's right! Always right!"

Kathy Bloomingdale 26 September 2011 at 11:29 [Report]

More sarcasm.

Madeline Cain 26 September 2011 at 11:44

Kathy 2, Claire 0.

"Why do you always listen to everyone else and never to yourself?"

I stared at her, mouth open, rant momentarily forgotten.

"My Dad taught me that. *You're smart, you're curious, you're brave,* he used to say. *Why would you listen to what anyone else thinks you should be? They're not you, not even your parents.* And he was right."

I was surprised Claire didn't hear my teeth grinding in the silence as she leant back against the window.

"I bet you've always done what's expected of you. Being a good girl, following the paths others set for you. But it's only making you unhappy. You need your small moments of rebellion, like your friend Kathy, daring to do something her mother doesn't like, working within the rules but to her own ends, not anyone else's. And when she's ready, the big rebellion will happen, and sure her parents might be upset, but they'll realise they actually knew this was going to happen all along because Kathy laid those seeds. You need to stop being a regular sheep and start growing some black wool. If you could do anything you wanted, without anyone giving you any information on why you couldn't, what would it be?"

I knew where she was trying to lead me. I knew she wanted me to be shocked by the straight forward words and say 'photography'. But I was so incensed at her misunderstanding me, at her own belief that I was just a *sheep,* that I let her have it.

Kathy Bloomingdale 26 September 2011 at 11:45 [Report]

Oh Mad, she was just trying to help.

Madeline Cain 26 September 2011 at 11:45

I'm NOT a sheep!

Kathy Bloomingdale 26 September 2011 at 11:46 [Report]

I know you're not, honey. And when you explain to her exactly why you reacted the way you did I'm sure she'll feel stupid in turn and you'll be able to make up.

Madeline Cain 26 September 2011 at 11:56

I'm not so sure about that, you see, this is how it went down:

"Well la–de–da, look who has a Dad who actually lets her have some autonomy, who actually allows her to make decisions and not put her under house arrest. Bet your Dad just laughed and waved you on the aeroplane with zero tears, happy in the knowledge that you were going to Australia so you could weird people out at check-in counters. Have one big bloody adventure and not have to worry about the future. Isn't it so great that you have a perfect bloody Dad? Hey here's an idea, why don't we swap and see how well you go with my Mum? I'll tell your Dad I'm off to make daisy chains in Canada or something else to avoid life."

Hands on hips I pulled in huge gulps of air while Claire looked at me completely expressionless.

"Well that would be a bit hard, my Dad's dead."

Kathy Bloomingdale 26 September 2011 at 11:56 [Report]

Shit.

Madeline Cain 26 September 2011 at 12:04

Yep, Shit.

I took a step back and knocked myself onto my own bed. "I…"

"He died about six months ago. Doing fun things used to be our thing, each day out was something different. So I decided that I would do something fun every day for a year to honour him. To show him how much I missed him."

She looked up at the ceiling and I think she was blinking back tears. I've never felt like such a dinosaur turd before. It was horrible.

Claire shrugged her shoulders. "The first thing I did was book an exchange to Australia. So now you know, the big event that started it all." She cleared her throat. "I should go. I'll check my phone every day from now on, yeah? So we don't get caught out again or, whatever. Sorry. "

Silence filled the room and I couldn't think of a single thing to say that would make this whole conversation just go away. What do you do when a girl confessed to letting you do something with her that she'd only ever done with her dead father?

Kathy Bloomingdale 26 September 2011 at 12:06 [Report]

You stop being a dinosaur turd and apologise! From everything you've told me she seems like she wouldn't hold a grudge, she could see how upset you were, she'll respond well to an apology and will probably offer one of her own. I would.

Madeline Cain 26 September 2011 at 12:07

She was being sarcastic Kath, she wants me to call as much as she wants her father resurrected from the grave as a clown.

Kathy Bloomindale 26 September 2011 at 12:09 [Report]

Your pride is crowding that itty bitty brain of yours, it was an olive branch she was extending. An awkward one, yes, but only because she was trying to avoid the Pity Train she thought was coming her way from station Madeline.

Madeline Cain 26 September 2011 at 12:10

You think so? I really can't think of anyone else I'd rather sneak out of my house with. Except you of course. And maybe Tim. In a pinch.

Kathy Bloomingdale 26 September 2011 at 12:11 [Report]

I really have to meet this replacement of mine. Either we'd get along, or I'd have to kill her.

Madeline Cain 26 September 2011 at 12:12

I'm gonna go option one. But if it comes to option two my bet is on Tim getting caught in the cross-fire and dying. It's the way he'd want to go, between two hot women.

Kathy Bloomingdale 26 September 2011 at 12:13 [Report]

Awww, you say the nicest things. So, are you still going to pull this application together? Or am I going to have to punish you for making me sit through an hour PM session with your brother for nothing.

Madeline Cain 26 September 2011 at 12:16

Please, no more punishments! Unless it involves me having to eat my way out of a vat of chocolate.

Yes, I'll do it, I need this. That is, if I can get the right people on board to help, I'll do it. I can't sneak out of Fort Mum on my own. Currently, the list of passable sidekicks only has Tim on it. I'm gonna have to dust off the *I'm a wanker* flag and try and get in contact with Claire somehow, probably through passable sidekick Tim.

Kathy Bloomingdale 26 September 2011 at 12:18 [Report]

A sad state of affairs. Look, you probably wouldn't have to fly that flag at all if you say sorry to Claire by doing some covert DoF under the nose of your jailers. "I was a jackass, please accept my contribution to your cause."

Madeline Cain 26 September 2011 at 12:19

And offer her a choice of forgiving me, or making me do a Days of Fun idea that I vetoed in the past.

Kathy Bloomingdale 26 September 2011 at 12:19 [Report]

Like?

Madeline Cain 26 September 2011 at 12:20

Like using me as a battering ram to knock down small children pretending to be bowling pins.

Kathy Bloomingdale 26 September 2011 at 12:20 [Report]

That's the spirit!

Tim Gleeve How is no one selling this as the cure-all for the un-dateable nerd? I must patent this immediately! I'll be a millionaire! And no you can't know what it is I've discovered. No one can know. There's no such thing as planning security too early when potential mobs of Christian House-Mums with placards is in the near future. *Posted Monday 26th September at 13:25* [Comment . Like]

> **Kathy Bloomingdale** What are you planning? Christian Girls Gone Nerd or some other weird TV show spin off? *Posted Monday 26th September at 13:37* [Comment . Like]

Madeline Cain Oh my god! Tim, do you have no shame? How could you write this on a paper aeroplane and throw this through my window?? This was like getting a cattle brand of a penis to the face! What if my mum saw it? Wait until Kathy finds out. *Posted Monday 26th September at 13:42* [Comment . Like]

Tim Gleeve Kathy has her own digital aeroplane waiting for her. Now remember, that non-disclosure clause on the wing of the plane is iron clad legal. You gave your agreement to tell *no one* when you unfolded it to read the message. Repeat after me *NO ONE*. Not even if threatened with your great aunt's fruit cake. *Posted Monday 26th September at 13:46* [Comment . Like]

Madeline Cain I don't want people trying this at home. I don't want visions of *you* trying this at home! *Posted Monday 26th September at 13:47* [Comment . Like]

Kathy Bloomingdale Eeew, Tim, no! What is wrong with you? Don't patent. I repeat don't patent. Abort. Abort!! *Posted Monday 26th September at 13:48* [Comment . Like]

Madeline Cain I'll keep your dirty little secret Tim, but only if you help me get a message to Claire. *Posted Monday 26th September at 13:49* [Comment . Like]

Tim Gleeve That's not how non-disclosure clauses work. But I'm a reasonable guy, I can do messages. *Posted Monday 26th September at 13:50* [Comment . Like]

Madeline Cain That's what I thought. *Posted Monday 26th September at 13:51* [Comment . Like]

Kyle Traybna I just marathon watched the Highlander movies and I'm pretty sure my internal voice is now Scottish. *Posted Tuesday 27th September at 18:02* [Comment . Like]

Tim Gleeve Aye! I suppose next you'll be asking for 'kips' on my couch. *Posted Tuesday 27th September at 18:23* [Comment . Like]

Kyle Traybna I need to buy tartan. *Posted Tuesday 27th September at 18:34* [Comment . Like]

Virginia Lowe Death is only the end if you assume the story is about you. *Posted Wednesday 28th September at 11:44* [Comment . Like]

Tim Gleeve Very meta. *Posted Wednesday 28th September at 11:50* [Comment . Like]

Virginia Lowe Why are you still alive? *Posted Wednesday 28th September at 11:53* [Comment . Like]

Tim Gleeve You try to compliment a girl and then BAM they knock you out with a Greenpeace pamphlet. *Posted Wednesday 28th September at 11:56* [Comment . Like]

Kathy Bloomingdale likes the page **Sometimes I Tell Myself I Have Insomnia, When Truthfully I Have A Good Book And An Inadequate Respect For Tomorrow.** [Like]

Madeline Cain Played the 'I need my tutor's phone number card' to get my phone back. When it comes to this, I have no shame. *Pets phone, goes back to work*. *Posted Thursday 29th September at 16:15* [Comment . Like]

Tim Gleeve –> Madeline Cain Claire made me send you this 365 DoF report. She wants me to relay that we walked up to a McDonald's counter, told the server, "Dude, the Maltesers are coming. And they have cross-bows." Then we ran away. End Report. *Posted Friday 30th September at 19:24* [Comment . Like]

Madeline Cain Thanks… I think… *Posted Friday 30th September at 19:40* [Comment . Like]

Tim Gleeve That's what he said. *Posted Friday 30th September at 19:43* [Comment . Like]

Madeline Cain First of Oct, the first day of holidays and the first day of official incarceration by sergeant major Nadine Cain. But jail time or no, nothing can stop the resourceful Madeline Cain from getting in her own day of fun! If only I didn't have to wait three days for it to appear in the newspaper. *Posted Saturday 1st October at 11:12* [Comment . Like]

Tim Gleeve –> Kathy Bloomingdale Happy birthday old girl. Congratulations on being the first of us to reach the age where you can now be sent to adult prison. *Posted Saturday 1st October at 12:00* [Comment . Like]

Madeline Cain –> Kathy Bloomingdale Can't believe you're celebrating your big one eight on the other side of the world! Happy birthday lovely lady. I hope you find a nice rainbow so you can slide down and power slam the cheeky bastard at the bottom who's hording all that gold. *Posted Saturday 1st October at 13:13* [Comment . Like]

Kathy Bloomingdale –> Madeline Cain I hope we're friends until we die. Then I hope we stay ghost friends and walk through walls and scare the shit out of people. *Posted Saturday 1st October at 20:20* [Comment . Like]

> **Madeline Cain** Are you... are you drunk? *Posted Saturday 1st October at 20:42* [Comment . Like]

> **Kathy Bloomingdale** Am not! YOU'RE durnk. *Posted Saturday 1st October at 20:50* [Comment . Like]

> **Madeline Cain** Oh dear. *Posted Saturday 1st October at 20:52* [Comment . Like]

Kathy Bloomingdale Guinness is where taste buds go to die. That is all. *Posted Sunday 2nd October at 12:30* [Comment . Like]

Madeline Cain So that was *Guinness* laced posting you were doing last night. It must have been pretty good. *Posted Sunday 2nd October at 12:43* [Comment . Like]

Kathy Bloomingdale It tastes like beer poured into an ashtray and then left stagnant for several months. But then again, this is my first beer, so maybe they all taste like bitter disappointment and poor oral hygiene. *Posted Sunday 2nd October at 12:52* [Comment . Like]

Madeline Cain Update #22, 365 Days of Fun: Today I got a very excited phone call, and made an effusive apology (and graciously received one) after 100,000 copies of this classified ad hit the streets today:

Evil Genius and Future Overlord of Planet Earth *requires minions for world domination. Must be prepared to sacrifice lives and work 24/7 for no pay with a psychopath. Potential to go back in time but safety is not guaranteed. Will provide minions with death rays and costumes to make up for inevitable messy death. No nutcases. Call: 13-EV-IL*

Posted Sunday 2nd October at 10:42 [Comment . Like]

Kate Nikles likes the page **Coffee: A Warm, Delicious Alternative To Hating Everybody, Every Morning, Forever.** [Like]

Mike Cain As expected, the subject did not do the proper checks when leaving the house. Mission initiated. *Posted Monday 3rd October at 10:17* [Comment . Like]

Mike Cain The subject is still oblivious, and there's barely enough cover for a relevant tail. How the subject has survived this long without getting assassinated, we'll never know. *Posted Monday 3rd October at 10:43* [Comment . Like]

Mike Cain The subject is clearly confused about the appropriate accessories for a sunny day. *Posted Monday 3rd October at 10:55* [Comment . Like]

Mike Cain Subject has acquired a target. Missiles have been locked and are awaiting orders. Once the area is cleared the trap will be set. *Posted Monday 3rd October at 11:29* [Comment . Like]

Mike Cain If I had a bow and arrow right now, I'd not be able to resist the temptation of letting one loose at the subject's bottom. It's taunting me. *Posted Monday 3rd October at 11:32* [Comment . Like]

Mike Cain Uh-oh. Have been spotted by one of the smarter of the subject's entourage. Operation Hide In A Tree initiated. *Posted Monday 3rd October at 11:43* [Comment . Like]

Shades Of Joy, OR, The Demise Of A Friend [New Message]

[Back to messages. Mark as unread . Report spam . Delete]

Between **Kathy Bloomingdale, Tim Gleeve** and **You.**

Madeline Cain 3 October 2011 at 19:13

I've had the best, the worst and the weirdest of days and it's driving me nuts that I can't post this publically because of you-know-who and his perchance for throwing me under the bus.

Kathy Bloomindale 3 October 2011 at 19:20 [Report]

Voldemort? ? There's a simple solution to that. It's called defriending your brother.

Madeline Cain 3 October 2011 at 19:23

That's like waving a red flag at a dozen bulls. He'd know something was up. This way, it stays in the family.

Tim Gleeve 3 October 2011 at 19:24 [Report]

I like how we're referred to as family and your actual family are just 'people I sometimes pass in the hallway'.

Kathy Bloomingdale 3 October 2011 at 19:25 [Report]

I feel like I'm missing something.

Madeline Cain 3 October 2011 at 19:27

You've missed *several* things. You missed that comment. You missed the wink Tim gave me when we met down the street from my house as he munched on a piece of toast. And, you missed the look of horror on his face when he realised he'd accidentally confessed to not getting detention, but spending his spare hours collecting butterflies.

Tim Gleeve 3 October 2011 at 19:28 [Report]

Hey! At least I didn't go into epic meltdown mode when my crummy red umbrella couldn't hack a mild weather event.

Madeline Cain 3 October 2011 at 19:29

Mild weather event?? It was a *hail storm*! And that wasn't just some crummy umbrella. Laani was my beautiful and faithful friend.

Kathy Bloomingdale 3 October 2011 at 19:30 [Report]

Oh no! Laani the umbrella is no more?? What happened?

Tim Gleeve 3 October 2011 at 19:31 [Report]

Girls are weird. It's not a person! It's a personal weather repellent. What is it with chicks? You'll give any old piece of junk a name.

Madeline Cain 3 October 2011 at 19:33

Says the man that gave his willy a first, last *and* middle name. She was not junk. Something with such delicately carved swirls in her wooden handle and such opulent red ruffles could never be junk. We were ambushed by the weather, Kathy. It conspired to rip Laani from my fingers, flip her inside out and break every metallic spoke in her poor, defenceless body. I did not take it well.

Tim Gleeve 3 October 2011 at 19:38 [Report]

That's the understatement of the century. The way you screamed, I thought a close family member had been disembowelled and then fed to a chipmunk. It was like a badly scripted Hollywood drama.

"WHY!? Why?? You can't do this to me! I'll give you anything! The skin off my back, my mint condition 90's music collection, MY SOUL. No!? Nothing? No apology, no steam punk time machine, no demon with an agreement made of iron? Well fruit salad you Universe! Let's see how you go when I set your world on fire! Please! Please! Bring her back! Oh what a world!"

Then she melted into a puddle of sludge. She's actually in a beaker next to me right now dictating her responses, making my fingers dance to her tune even as a liquid. Because she has no hands. If you didn't get that part. Also, she said a naughty word instead of 'fruit salad', if you missed that too.

Kathy Bloomingdale 3 October 2011 at 19:44 [Report]

You're a subtle as a sledge hammer to the crown jewels my friend, even a cabbage would have picked that up.

I'm so sorry, Maddie, I know she was your favourite possession. But at least Laani died for a noble cause, in the pursuit of her mistress's happy ending.

That came out dirtier than I intended it.

What I mean is, she would be proud, nay honoured, to be instrumental in the creation of the application which will open the gate to your future career and life passion.

I did get that right didn't I? You *were* sneaking out of the house to take the photos for your application for Jason's course? You weren't like, proving your black sheep-ness by doing a jail break to ride a dinosaur rollercoaster or anything? Not that I would blame you, dinosaurs are awesome.

Madeline Cain 3 October 2011 at 19:45

They are, but not as awesome as making my Shades of Fun project a reality. It was scary and thrilling and at times I wanted to pee my pants rather than approach a person to ask for their permission to use the photo.

Kathy Bloomingdale 3 October 2011 at 19:46 [Report]

Where did you end up doing it?

Madeline Cain 3 October 2011 at 20:00

In Adelaide Botanic Park. It was the first warm day since last summer so there were picnic blankets set up everywhere, children chasing (or being chased by) ducks, and so many poorly played ball-related games I thought offering Tim to coach them like an Xbox FIFA team might actually improve the situation.

We wandered through the blushing rose gardens, across the pine covered greens near the weird, shell-like glasshouse, and made our way to a little patch of lawn next to a pool full of lotus and lily pads where I found the most perfect of subjects, a young expectant mother with a gentle smile and a far away look. I stood just far enough back to not be noticed and snapped away with my zoom lens. Claire hovered Laani over the two of us, blocking the more intense sunlight and reducing my lens flare, and also stopping her delicate white skin from turning into a parody of a lobster.

When it came to approach the woman to sign the release form, I instead confused the hell out of her as I tried and failed to collect the right words for my request. It was only when Claire took over with her fully formed sentences and reasonable words guiding the woman through the photo release process, that I realised Tim was nowhere to be found. At first I thought he had gone to wiz in the bamboo, but when five minutes, then ten passed I started to imagine wilder and wilder scenarios and Claire and I started searching for him in earnest. Could he have tripped and drowned in the lily pads? Been kidnapped by a bunch of fun-hating fundamentalists? Abandoned me in pursuit of a hot girl he would only be slapped by?

Then just as suddenly as he disappeared he remerged behind us, scaring the shit-kittens out of me.

"Looking for me?"

I whorled around to face him. "Where the bloody hell have you been?"

He shrugged, looking uncomfortable. "Oh, you know."

"No I don't know! Where have you been, we've wasted twenty minutes of daylight looking for you!"

"Every minute you hold us up is a minute Madeline could get caught and then incarcerated like a dancing bear in a Russian circus," added Claire giving Tim her trademark, unblinking stare.

No matter how strong a man is, no matter how many torturous hours he has survived in hormone charged female company, or levels he's reached on World of Warcraft, no man can prepare for that penetrating gaze. No man can survive its weight without breaking.

You could see the sweats break out, the eyes darting from side to side, the nervous thumbing of the nose. Then he broke. Not with confessions of wooing girls in the bushes, or climbing trees, or stealing Frisbees from little children but with this:

"I was… Iwascollectingbutterflies! Ok?!"

Tim Gleeve 3 October 2011 at 20:03

You know Maddie, there are many things that should never be allowed a comeback tour: Nickleback; the Backstreet Boys; Justin Bieber in ten years; flared disco pants; Rubik cubes; Fluoro colours; or the word 'Groovy'. The knowledge of my recreational habits is one of those things. Bury the knowledge deep in your psyche, never to surface again.

Madeline Cain 3 October 2011 at 20:04

In the same place as the 'I told you so' that I was saving up for your birthday suit related incident the other day?

Tim Gleeve 3 October 2011 at 20:05

The very same.

Kathy Bloomingdale 3 October 2011 at 20:10

Oh my god I thought you were joking before! Like, haha Tim and his birthday suit toast and other imaginary fetishes (I cannot, for a moment believe that toaster story Tim. It is without a doubt the most made up story I've ever heard. You used some sort of internet phrase generator on some adult porn site. I know you did!).

But he actually *collects butterflies?* For real? And not only collects them but *gives himself imaginary detention* so he can do said collecting? Skips out on side splitting tarot card readings to hang with caterpillars?

Is that why you cocooned yourself in a full bodied lycra suit for your superhero outing? You wanted to turn into a beautiful butterfly?

Tim Gleeve 3 October 2011 at 20:12

Fine! Yes, I spend my time searching for the most delicate of God's flying creatures, but that does not make me a pansy, or a nerd or *shudder* a greenie. I'm a man! A man who hunts and covers his walls in trophies.

Madeline Cain 3 October 2011 at 20:18

Yes rainbow coloured trophies. No antlers or horns for you, just fairy wings.

Like Pandora's box, once the truth was out, there was no way we were stuffing it back in. Tim put his fetish on full display, much to the delight of Claire who had clearly decided Tim was to be her fun for the day.

Like a magician, he pulled a bag full of pink powdered chalk from his pocket and proceeded at every photographic stop we made to mark the ground where he thought good 'butterfly breeding zones' were. When we were on the grass he'd drop a whole handful of the stuff and start grounding it into the lawn with his foot as though afraid it would float away on a stray breeze and render all of this strenuous walking useless.

You should've seen how ape-shit he went when Claire managed to get her hand in the chalk bag and start throwing handfuls at random spots on the lawn. Apparently breaking me out of the house was just an excuse to spend the day roaming through the garden without being flagged by police as a potential risk to children.

Tim Gleeve 3 October 2011 at 20:20

She was interfering in a delicate science! And yes, I may have been there for an alternative purpose but the intentions behind my assistance in your jailbreak were pure. You too are a delicate butterfly Maddie, you shouldn't be caged. Or mounted on a wall in a hypobarically sealed box.

Madeline Cain 3 October 2011 at 20:22

Gee, thanks. I don't know why it bothered you, it seems like this whole botanic park is a sex dungeon for the species anyway. There were as many 'breeding zones' as there were photos I took. And that was a LOT. It's probably why you're attracted to them, they're as randy as you are.

Kathy Bloomingdale 3 October 2011 at 20:23

I have the best image of Tim prancing around throwing handfuls of pink chalk at trees, children and park officials. And then humping cocoons. Which is kind of disturbing.

Tim Gleeve 3 October 2011 at 20:24

So what? I've an unusual hobby and suddenly it proves I'm into bestiality? I'm offended!

Kathy Bloomingdale 3 October 2011 at 20:25

That's nice. Can your new super-name be Butterfly Boy?

Madeline Cain 3 October 2011 at 20:25

Yes!

Tim Gleeve 3 October 2011 at 20:29

No! No Butterfly Boy, or Pink Fairies, or Polka Dot Llamas. It's Super Tim, Man of Awesome. This will never change. Never!

Now let's move back to the real story here. The story of one brave Madeline who has faced being confined in her room by her mother for life. She's the real hero of this story. Or the real idiot, because rather than doing the smart thing and taking a dozen photos and getting her butt back up the vertical obstacle course to her window after an hour, she instead decided to risk a whole five hours to take ten million photos of strangers in a park.

Madeline Cain 3 October 2011 at 20:39

Don't think I didn't see what you did there! Deflecting the conversation from your weirdness. I'm watching you and we'll be revisiting this odd behaviour soon...

He's exaggerating Kathy, I only took photos of two dozen people, then I'll be picking six photos from that for the application. I wanted as large a range of joy as possible, so I had to take dozens of photos to get the right angle. It felt like we were paparazzi spying on the rich being normal. At the end of the day the photos were getting harder and harder to take as the clouds started rolling through and the light began to dim and the picnickers began scrambling to pack up their gear. It wasn't until a crack of thunder and a stiff breeze blew through that I realised the weather had throw the storm switch. It went from full sun to full gale in half an hour.

Then came that fateful moment when Claire almost blew off into the sky like Merry Poppins and I snatched Laani from her grasp only to have my poor umbrella jump from my fingers and twirl away into the paths under the trees. Thankfully the camera was already stowed in its waterproof pouch. It allowed me to belt after her.

Tim Gleeve 3 October 2011 at 20:40

Yelling obscenities like a sailor.

Madeline Cain 3 October 2011 at 20:50

Cursing the world like a lady, only to come face to face with a red faced Mike, my darling Laani crushed in his hands. I shrieked and pounced on him, giving him a big wet kiss on the cheek. He flinched and when I stepped back he was watching me wide-eyed and weary.

I hugged poor broken Laani to my chest and stared at him in confusion, finally realising why it was so weird to see him there. He was as grounded as I was. What the hell was he doing out of the house?

"Why are you here Mike?"

I didn't think it was possible but his eyes widened even further. "Uh."

"If you're spying on me…" I started, my voice as deep, growly and threatening as I could make it.

"No! No, I came to warn you! Mum is planning a date night with Dad and if you're not home quick smart you're going to *not* be in your room when she comes to force brother-sitting duty on you."

That's when it started to hail. You get out of parks pretty quick smart regardless after that.

Kathy Bloomingdale 3 October 2011 at 20:52

If Mike already tracked you to the park (you're lucky he's so nosey and listens into your phone conversations on the extra house phone) why exactly can't you post a public ode to a successful day's photography and a friend's weird obsession?

Madeline Cain 3 October 2011 at 20:53

Because I live in hope that my brother won't do anything about this knowledge unless I remind him, and if he does, it will just be his word against mine with no written evidence!

Kathy Bloomingdale 3 October 2011 at 20:55

You know, it's not often you can say this about Mike, but sometimes, he's a good brother. Also, he probably doesn't want your mother to know he performed a bit of jailbreak to come tell you.

Tim on the other hand will always be that weird almost-brother that we kind of got stuck with. Miss ya, Tim :p

Tim Gleeve 3 October 2011 at 20:57

First you stab me in the heart and then you cover me in emoticons. Typical. Trust me Maddie. That boy doesn't need blackmail to have his fun. Mark my words.

Madeline Cain 3 October 2011 at 20:58

With pink chalk? Or is that just for butterfly sex zones?

Tim Gleeve 3 October 2011 at 20:59

Uuugh! Why did I leave my house today??

———

Tim Gleeve To the person on the internet who decided that 'Pink fluffy unicorns dancing on rainbows' was a thing. I HATE you. *Posted Monday 3rd October at 22:22* [Comment . Like]

> **Madeline Cain** Finally found a part of the internet you don't like? *Posted Monday 3rd October at 22:36* [Comment . Like]
>
> **Tim Gleeve** It's like falling into a deep black hole only to be attacked by My Little Ponies. *Posted Monday 3rd October at 22:48* [Comment . Like]

Mike Cain Subject remains blissfully unaware of the secret project that will save her boring bacon. Have been out three times now while she unknowingly holds the fort. *Posted Tuesday 4th October at 09:40* [Comment . Like]

Lulu Tanaki likes the page **Babysitters Don't Actually Sit On Babies.** [Like]

Tim GleeveMadeline Cain 365 DoF Report: Today, while some poor city shmuck was swimming at Glenelg, two certain someones stole the clothes this swimmer left on the beach, leaving behind replacement clothing of an unusual nature... *Posted Tuesday 4th October at 19:20* [Comment . Like]

> **Kathy Bloomingdale** Please don't say it was a shell bikini and mermaid tail. *Posted Tuesday 4th October at 19:41* [Comment . Like]
>
> **Tim Gleeve** Sadly no. It required a personal sacrifice on my part for the greater laughs. *Posted Tuesday 4th October at 19:47* [Comment . Like]
>
> **Madeline Cain** Ah! You left them your superhero costume! *Posted Tuesday 4th October at 19:50* [Comment . Like]
>
> **Tim Gleeve** Alas, yes. Literal Man is now a very pissed off businessman stalking back to his car. *Posted Tuesday 4th October at 19:53* [Comment . Like]

Mike Cain The subject almost caught me in the middle of preparing the project. Must take extra precautions to not show my hand before the time is ready. *Posted Wednesday 5th October at 13:18* [Comment . Like]

Virginia Lowe The biggest communication problem is we do not listen to understand. We listen to reply. *Posted Wednesday 5th October at 15:37* [Comment . Like]

> **Tim Gleeve** Totally! What could be better than everyone hearing my opinion? Actually, that's easy. Hearing my opinion and agreeing with it. *Posted Wednesday 5th October at 15:40* [Comment . Like]

> **Virginia Lowe** Generation Y, case in point. *Posted Wednesday 5th October at 15:43* [Comment . Like]

> **Tim Gleeve** You and sarcasm have never been introduced, have you, Vee? *Posted Wednesday 5th October at 15:50* [Comment . Like]

Mike Cain Alternative narrative has been completed after much complex Photoshopping. Now to slip the final cogs into place at the very last moment! *Posted Thursday 6th October at 23:04* [Comment . Like]

Kathy Bloomingdale Holy shit. I made it. I MADE IT! I now have a certificate and a little hand written note from the Head of the course commending me on my stellar performance. I've made *clothes*, with my *hands*. They were in my imagination and now they're real! It's like magic that takes six weeks and four hours sleep a night. It is glorious!!! *Posted Friday 7th October at 14:07* [Comment . Like]

> **Madeline Cain** Congratulations beautiful girl! Now you're in holiday mode too! The only difference between the two of us is you can actually go somewhere other than your room. *Posted Friday 7th October at 14:13* [Comment . Like]

Kathy Bloomingdale I'll go all the places for you, Maddie! Could you pass on my apologies to future you for taking such horrible holiday photographs? *Posted Friday 7th October at 14:17* [Comment . Like]

Madeline Cain Only if that pre-ordered straight jacket is among your new cloth-made possessions. *Posted Friday 7th October at 14:25* [Comment . Like]

Kathy Bloomingdale We did a horror movie component in week three ? It's in the bag. Literally. *Posted Friday 7th October at 14:31* [Comment . Like]

Mike Cain Subject is spending thirty minutes in the shower completely unaware that her hardware is not secure. Project now complete. Launch imminent. *Posted Saturday 8th October at 08:40* [Comment . Like]

Madeline Cain Submitted! My submission to Jason's NYC course is out in the internet void creating possibilities. I don't know whether to do a happy dance or puke. *Posted Saturday 8th October at 11:40* [Comment . Like]

Kathy Bloomingdale Irish high-five! *Posted Saturday 8th October at 12:08* [Comment . Like]

Tim Gleeve What does that even look like? Do you have a Guinness in your hand and bump fists? Draw a four leaf clover on your palm? Dance an Irish gig while trying to high five without slapping the other person in the face? *Posted Saturday 8th October at 12:12* [Comment . Like]

Kathy Bloomingdale You're right, I didn't think that one through. *Posted Saturday 8th October at 12:17* [Comment . Like]

Isabelle Haigh Today my cat Othello celebrates his 5th birthday. Well when I say 'celebrates' I mean it's work as usual. But if he does a good job mowing the lawn I'll give him some cake. *Posted Sunday 9th October at 10:18* [Comment . Like]

Diana Lynal What is it with men!? It's always excuses, excuses followed by 'something-something our-poor-penises'. *Posted Monday 10th October at 19:05* [Comment . Like]

> **Madeline Cain** Are you alright? *Posted Monday 10th October at 19:14* [Comment . Like]

> **Tim Gleeve** Another one bites the dust. *Posted Monday 10th October at 19:19* [Comment . Like]

> **Madeline Cain** It's called being unlucky in love, Timothy. You wouldn't understand, your closest encounter has been with an electrical appliance. *Posted Monday 10th October at 19:28* [Comment . Like]

Madeline Cain Today we do inside activities. Again. *head desk*. *Posted Tuesday 11th October at 10:12* [Comment . Like]

> **Kathy Bloomingdale** I thought you had to make up for all the school work you 'missed'? *Posted Tuesday 11th October at 11:24* [Comment . Like]

> **Madeline Cain** I finished that after, like, three days. *Posted Tuesday 11th October at 11:31* [Comment . Like]

> **Tim Gleeve** Your brain is wasted on you. *Posted Tuesday 11th October at 11:50* [Comment . Like]

Wyate Yosime likes the page **Microsoft Word Will Never Understand That My Name Is NOT A Spelling Mistake.** [Like]

Ray Star So apparently our little one is totally up to speed in the tracking objects and sounds department. So while it's too early to tell if he's the next DaVinci, he's certainly no cabbage. *Posted Wednesday 12th October at 14:35* [Comment . Like]

Madeline Cain Update #33, 365 Days of Fun: Sneak in an activity behind your Mother's back. This can be achieved by going to the dentist, standing behind your Mother in the elevator and doing the Macarena while other patrons get on. *Posted Thursday 13th October at 15:12* [Comment . Like]

> **Tim Gleeve** Heeeeeyyyyyy Macarena. Ei! *Posted Thursday 13th October at 16:30* [Comment . Like]
>
> **Kathy Bloomingdale** Sounds like it would be less fun having to mouth the words. *Posted Thursday 13th October at 16:55* [Comment . Like]
>
> **Madeline Cain** On the contrary, initial reactions were more comical than first expected. *Posted Thursday 13th October at 17:05* [Comment . Like]

Kathy Bloomingdale likes the page **Instead Of 'Have A Nice Day' I Think I'll Start Saying 'Have The Day You Deserve'. You Know, Let Karma Sort That Shit Out.** [Like]

Harry Lee I got my new hoodie today. And let me tell you, it's softer than the tresses of Jesus. *Posted Thursday 13th October at 18:10* [Comment . Like]

Madeline Cain OH MY GOD! I can't breathe! I can't breathe. I got in. I. GOT. IN! *Posted Friday 14th October at 09:44* [Comment . Like]

> **Madeline Cain** Holy shit. Now I have to tell my mother. Oh god oh god oh god. *Posted Friday 14th October at 09:47* [Comment . Like]
>
> **Tim Gleeve** I get the feeling that the Oh Gods in those two sentences were for entirely different reasons. Oh, and congratulations on running away from me. You're so lucky you and Kathy are tag teaming or I'd have to take measures... *Posted Friday 14th October at 10:12* [Comment . Like]

Kathy Bloomingdale No shit Sherlock. Wow Maddie, that's the best news ever! But also the worst news ever. These last six weeks have been torture being away from you. How am I going to do twelve months?? It's been less than a week since you handed it in, how come you got a response back so quickly? *Posted Friday 14th October at 10:20* [Comment . Like]

Madeline Cain They let me know early based on the 'strength of my application'. Which is amazing, but at the same time – Mum. She went ape-shit during her lecture the other day about what she thought about people without uni degrees. *Posted Friday 14th October at 10:24* [Comment . Like]

Tim Gleeve You've got to tell her. *Posted Friday 14th October at 10:27* [Comment . Like]

Madeline Cain Captain Obvious strikes again. *Posted Friday 14th October at 10:28* [Comment . Like]

Facing The Family Firing Squad [New Message]

[Back to messages. Mark as unread . Report spam . Delete]

Between **Kathy Bloomingdale, Tim Gleeve** and **You.**

Kathy Bloomingdale 14 October 2011 at 19:19 [Report]

How did the talk go? Are you still in one piece? Your Mum didn't do what my Mum did, did she? Shriek and collapse on the floor?

Tim Gleeve 14 October 2011 at 19:27 [Report]

Do you now have your name carved into the door of your very own dungeon? A custom made ball and chain?

Madeline Cain 14 October 2011 at 19:29

Noooo, the whole thing was... odd, so odd. My Mum is... *weird.* I don't understand how her brain works. You think she's going to do one thing then BAM she does the complete opposite.

Kathy Bloomingdale 14 October 2011 at 19:31 [Report]

So no seizures, fake or otherwise? No chaining you to a desk until you're enrolled in a science degree of her choice?

Tim Gleeve 14 October 2011 at 19:32 [Report]

No lame name or poorly made costuming choices that reveal the makings of a comic book supervillain?

Madeline Cain 14 October 2011 at 19:34

No. I spent a day of gathering courage, forming arguments, and creating my first handful of grey hair, and when I finally told her I was going to New York not to study science but photography... she *laughed.*

Tim Gleeve 14 October 2011 at 19:35 [Report]

Mayday, mayday! Abort! Abort! Psychopathic mother rant imminent.

Madeline Cain 14 October 2011 at 19:36

See that's what I thought! But she was just *happy.* Happy I had some sort of direction and ambition.

Tim Gleeve 14 October 2011 at 19:38 [Report]

What? I was hoping for a story where your Mum turned into some sort of Godzilla. Mumzilla! But instead I get a Brady Bunch episode. Quick make it more interesting, add sex robots or...or laser guns! Or sex robots WITH laser guns.

Madeline Cain 14 October 2011 at 19:39

I feel like that kitchen incident has flicked some weird switches in your brain...

Kathy Bloomingdale 14 October 2011 at 19:40 [Report]

Then why was she acting, like Mike articulated so well, like she had her panties caught in a panty tornado a couple of weeks ago?

Madeline Cain 14 October 2011 at 19:43

I asked her exactly the same thing!

She actually *flushed,* then crossing her arms around her stomach she said, "I was worried that if Daddy and I let it slide that you'd miss out on all your opportunities and become a bum, or get pregnant or become some sort of wandering hippy who lives off the sale of hash cookies."

Kathy Bloomingdale 14 October 2011 at 19:44 [Report]

I get the feeling there was more to your Mum's early 80's then she's letting on.

Tim Gleeve 14 October 2011 at 19:45 [Report]

My bet's on pot smoking sex robots. Imagine the psychedelic light shows.

Madeline Cain 14 October 2011 at 19:53

I don't know if I want to open *that* particular Pandora's box.

She knew what she said was ridiculous. I didn't even have to say anything, just look at her with raised eyebrows.

She gave an annoyed huff, throwing her hands wide. "Look, I know they were silly fears, but they all stemmed from that little devil in my head who told me I wasn't doing my job, I wasn't being a good enough parent, that I would botch up your future by not being firm."

"Hence the '1984' smack-down?"

"At least I didn't lock you in the cupboard under the stairs."

"Look at how far you've come," I shot back, and we shared a grin at the double meaning. My copy of the first Harry Potter book has been sitting on her bedside table for about a decade. Every time I try to claim it back she responds with, 'No! I'm not finished yet.'

She pulled me in for a hug and we sank down into the living room couch.

Tim Gleeve 14 October 2011 at 19:55 [Report]

And then a laser beam shot through the wall and speared Nadine through the head and cleaved her in two! Bricks and mortar exploded into the room and a sex robot strode through the giant hole, fully locked and loaded.

Madeline Cain 14 October 2011 at 19:56

No, niet, nein! Absolutely not! I'm willing to risk all sorts of space time paradoxes to go back in the past to gag you and avoid that comment.

Kathy Bloomingdale 14 October 2011 at 19:57 [Report]

Just ridicule the size of his non-existent penis, that will shut him up.

So you guys ended up hugging the last two weeks out. That's lovely.

Madeline Cain 14 October 2011 at 20:00

Frankly, it was a huge let down. I'd gotten myself all pumped to bring out Hulk Madeline and yell, "You're not the boss of me now!"

Then the nagging started. "Why couldn't you find your ambition closer to home? New York is so *far*." It was like I was suddenly speaking to a whining, nine year old Tim. Then I found myself promising I would call every week and only stay for a year and even set up a Facebook account for her so she could keep in touch every day.

Kathy Bloomingdale 14 October 2011 at 20:01 [Report]

Well that was stupid. Didn't you learn from the whole friending Mike thing?

Madeline Cain 14 October 2011 at 20:02

I know! I know! Sometimes I think she's more of an evil genius than him, lulling me into a false sense of security where I start making concessions I never should let out my mouth-hole.

Tim Gleeve 14 October 2011 at 20:03 [Report]

Now your Mum is going to see all of those naked volleyball pictures you posted.

Madeline Cain 14 October 2011 at 20:04

Only in your dreams. It figures that we would make up at the end of the holidays when I'd lost all my free time.

Kathy Bloomingdale 14 October 2011 at 20:06 [Report]

But it was worth it, look at how far you've come! You went after your dream when it seemed impossible and now you're going to the big apple! Who'd have thought that when you told a snooty university board where to shove their ping pong balls that you'd end up here?

Madeline Cain 14 October 2011 at 20:09

You know, you're the whole reason I did this. I was so *envious* of you, getting to have these adventures, being creative, actually having talent. But like a pumpkin I didn't *do* anything about it, I wasn't sure I had permission. Which was stupid. What time did I think we were living in? The middle ages? Were women suddenly walking around in corsets and organising a wedding to some man they'd only spoken to for half an hour? No!

Tim Gleeve 14 October 2011 at 20:10 [Report]

Shame. Corsets are hot.

Madeline Cain 14 October 2011 at 20:12

I realised I don't need permission. It's my life. I can choose to wear a corset or not, to go to uni or not, or do whatever the hell I want to do with my life. This weird obsession teachers and parents have with everyone going to university needs to stop.

Kathy Bloomingdale 14 October 2011 at 20:12 [Report]

Bravo!

Madeline Cain 14 October 2011 at 20:15

In saying that I did promise Mum that I wouldn't slack off on exams, 'just in case'. Just in case… well, I don't know what it's in case of. But if that's what I need to do to get her full support, I'll do it. Because as much as I no longer need permission, I'm still happy to get all the support I can. From what I understand, I'm going to need that support when things don't turn out the way I think it will. Right Kathy? ?

Kathy Bloomingdale 14 October 2011 at 20:16 [Report]

I'm nodding so hard right now it's like I'm a bobble-headed doll.

Tim Gleeve 14 October 2011 at 20:18 [Report]

Just in case New York City got blown up? Or Jason got eaten by a tiger before term started? Or every plane in the world suddenly forgot how to fly? Or robots started farming humans for sexy times? There are many practical reasons behind the request, Maddie. Use your imagination.

Madeline Cain 14 October 2011 at 20:20

I'm happy to use my imagination, but not in the same direction as you. Speaking of imagination, I got the weirdest bit of feedback back from that acceptance email Jason sent me. Maybe it comes from years of trying to interpret art. But he said that he and the judging panel, 'Loved the subtext' I apparently 'added' to the photo series, citing it as 'very powerful.' Wish I knew what he meant. Then I could do it on purpose!

Kathy Bloomingdale 14 October 2011 at 20:21 [Report]

I've been analysing films now for the past four weeks, flick the application to me and I'll see if I can figure out what he means.

Madeline Cain 14 October 2011 at 20:23

That would be awesome!

Just sent!

Maybe the subtext is the Shades of Joy part and they considered the main thing to be the portrait style.

Kathy Bloomingdale 14 October 2011 at 20:24 [Report]

Ah, Maddie, exactly how closely did you look at these photos?

Madeline Cain 14 October 2011 at 20:25

What do you mean how closely did I look at them? I edited them for, like, a week! I know every blade of bloody grass in them.

Kathy Bloomingdale 14 October 2011 at 20:27 [Report]

Yes, but have you looked at the photos you emailed me? Not the ones you've saved on your hard drive? Because there are some… interesting additions in the background thanks to what appears to be a rather dodgy invisible man.

Madeline Cain 14 October 2011 at 20:28

What? If there's an invisible man then how can you bloody see him?

Kathy Bloomingdale 14 October 2011 at 20:29 [Report]

Are you looking them up?

Madeline Cain 14 October 2011 at 20:30

Yes, yes! I'm downloading them but my internet connection is taking forever.

Kathy Bloomingdale 14 October 2011 at 20:35 [Report]

You can 'see' him because he's wearing gumboots, gloves, and a hat and tie. They are some *very* fluoro coloured accessories... I'm pretty sure they're a post production add because I don't see how you could have missed them when you were editing the shots. They stand out like a goth at a techno-rave. It completely changes the context of the photos.

There's this invisible man who, at first, looks like he's clowning around to make the people smile and laugh but actually it's a bit more...weird. He's holding a knife in one, sneaking up on that pregnant woman, and in another one of a balding guy belly laughing, the invisible man is juggling fire brands...

Madeline Cain 14 October 2011 at 20:37

What?!

I bet you I know exactly who's behind this. Fracken Michael! This has his stench all over it!

Argh!! Why are these only half downloaded! What else is there??

Kathy Bloomingdale 14 October 2011 at 20:39 [Report]

In another the invisible man is walking along with a shovel, then pretend choking himself, and then he appears to be pulling apart a stuffed dog... If I was on a judging panel I'd say they thought these beautiful laughing shots were just a mask covering the reality of that person's life represented by the invisible man bent on invisible destruction...

Madeline Cain 14 October 2011 at 20:42

Holy shit! How the hell did this happen!? Does Mike have some sort of green screen studio set up in his room that I don't know about?

WTF, is the invisible man wrestling with a pair of leopard print handcuffs in the last one??

Kathy Bloomingdale 14 October 2011 at 20:43 [Report]

Ah, you've managed to download them.

Madeline Cain 14 October 2011 at 20:45

In all their horrifying glory! Wait until I get my hands on Mike. I'm going to... cling wrap his room! I'm going to dye all of his clothes pink! I will fill his iPod with Disney songs and super glue his buds to his ears and his hands behind his back! He completely ruined everything!

Tim Gleeve 14 October 2011 at 20:46 [Report]

Did he though? Sounds like the panel loved his little addition. I feel like, maybe, you might have to thank him.

Madeline Cain 14 October 2011 at 20:48

As if! I'd rather lick a sloth!

Wait a minute. I know where I've seen those fluffy handcuffs before... During a certain unsuccessful citizens arrest! The invisible man is YOU! YOU HELPED RUIN MY APPLICATION!

Tim Gleeve 14 October 2011 at 20:49 [Report]

Whoa there Nellie, you got it wrong. I saved your photos. I cleverly talked your brother around to a less mischievous plan.

Madeline Cain 14 October 2011 at 20:50

YOU TALKED HIM AROUND TO A HOMICIDAL INVISIBLE MAN!?

Tim Gleeve 14 October 2011 at 20:51 [Report]

Sure did.

Madeline Cain 14 October 2011 at 20:51

HOW IS THAT A PLAN?!

Tim Gleeve 14 October 2011 at 20:57 [Report]

He was following you around the park with a much more drastic scheme in mind; he wanted to get identical photos with an empty landscape and use that to Photoshop everything out of *your* shots leaving only the laughing heads. It was going to end up like a Wizard of Oz parody. I don't think Jason and the panel would have connected with that particular theme.

So when I saw Mike in the park the other day, I cornered him. I demanded he tell me why he was following us with a bag of pink chalk or I would up end the bag over his head and turn him into a pink fairy princess.

He told me his dastardly scheme and I realised nothing would stop this bulldozer of naughtiness. It could only be deflected by one of great cunning, and skill. A chaperone who would monitor him at all times and see he did not default to his original plan and ruin his sister's future leaving her with only a career as a crazed chemist.

So I said unto him, "Do you want five minutes of fame, or do you want people to appreciate your genius."

And all was well.

Madeline Cain 14 October 2011 at 20:58

All will be well when I castrate you! And shove... flowers up your bum!

Tim Gleeve 14 October 2011 at 20:59 [Report]

How is it Mike is only threatened with Disney songs and I'm threatened with being turned into a eunuch and getting flower powered in the arse? Violence never changes the past, Maddie.

Kathy Bloomingdale 14 October 2011 at 21:02 [Report]

That's what the pink chalk was for! You were colluding with the enemy to mark where Maddie stood when she took her photos! I bet every butterfly 'breeding' zone was the exact location of one of her shots. No wonder you went ballistic when Claire started destroying your carefully planned trail. I can't believe Claire made you panic so much when you reappeared that you defaulted to an explanation of I'm collecting *butterflies!*

Tim Gleeve 14 October 2011 at 21:04 [Report]

It may have been panicked but it worked, didn't it? I only had to suffer a week or two of humiliation. I'd do it again! If only to save my friends from being too safe with their artwork and not getting the opportunities they deserve. That's the sort of sacrifice I'm willing to make for you guys.

Madeline Cain 14 October 2011 at 21:05

Bullshit! You did it because you're as much of a stirrer as my brother!

Tim Gleeve 14 October 2011 at 21:05 [Report]

You wound me!

Madeline Cain 14 October 2011 at 21:06

You're supposed to be on my side! What am I going to say when I first see Jason and he commends me on SOMETHING I DIDN'T DO??

Tim Gleeve 14 October 2011 at 21:10 [Report]

Correction, I am on the side of fun.

Do what I always do, claim the idea as your own. You said you wanted clever portfolio ideas and you went for the stock standard. Your brother is crazy, but I'm just trying to help a sister out. Just accept the good luck we generated on your behalf. You got a free ticket to NYC thanks to us.

Well, that and the original photos were a pretty awesome foreground to begin with. You've got a nice eye Mad, you'll do well in New York.

Kathy Bloomingdale 14 October 2011 at 21:11 [Report]

Suck up!

Tim Gleeve 14 October 2011 at 21:12 [Report]

It's all the truth.

Kathy Bloomingdale 14 October 2011 at 21:12 [Report]

Which part Butterfly Boy?

Tim Gleeve 14 October 2011 at 21:14 [Report]

Mad's a great photographer, I wanted to be in her photos for funsies, and I can redirect the destructive force of Brother Mike for good.

Also, and most importantly, I'm not a butterfly boy.

Kathy Bloomingdale 14 October 2011 at 21:15 [Report]

On the contrary, you are forevermore Butterfly Boy, Butterfly Boy.

Tim Gleeve 14 October 2011 at 21:16 [Report]

That's no way to treat this champion of friends! Frankly, I'm a genius. You girls don't pay me nearly enough to be your protector.

Madeline Cain 14 October 2011 at 21:17

I was almost at the point of forgiveness and then you said that. How is it that your version of events kind of makes sense but it still makes me want to bitch slap you?

Kathy Bloomingdale 14 October 2011 at 21:18 [Report]

It's his God-given gift.

Madeline Cain 14 October 2011 at 21:19

One he will pay for dearly with his new nickname, which I will give to Claire as a gift to thank her for setting me on my future path, and to punish Tim for interfering with it.

Tim Gleeve 14 October 2011 at 21:20 [Report]

Maddie, come on. Shouldn't we be punishing Mike? I can't help it if I was caught up in the steam roller of his plans.

Kathy Bloomingdale 14 October 2011 at 21:20 [Report]

Butterfly Boy.

Madeline Cain 14 October 2011 at 21:20

Butterfly Boy.

Tim Gleeve 14 October 2011 at 21:21 [Report]

Let's talk about this. Or better yet, let's just forget it all and go out for ice cream to celebrate. You know you don't want to start this new life of yours with rumours.

Madeline Cain 14 October 2011 at 21:22

Can invisible men hear, Bbbbbbbbbbbbbbbutterflyboy?

Kathy Bloomingdale 14 October 2011 at 21:23 [Report]

I'm just going to take a wild guess Madeline Cain Photographer Extraordinaire and say they can...

Tim Gleeve 14 October 2011 at 21:24 [Report]

Please don't.

Madeline Cain 14 October 2011 at 21:26

Butterfly Boy Butterfly Boy Butterfly Boy Butterfly Boy Butterfly Boy Butterfly Boy Butterfly Boy Butterfly Boy Butterfly Boy Butterfly Boy Butterfly Boy Butterfly Boy

---

Madeline Cain I'm so excited I could propel a rocket ship to Pluto on my happy dance. Kathy is home in TWO DAYS! Whee! *Posted Friday 14th October at 21:40* [Comment . Like]

> **Tim Gleeve** Then Kathy and Irish Kathy will meet and there will be an explosion of awesome. *Posted Friday 14th October at 21:52* [Comment . Like]

> **Madeline Cain** It'll be like a possum diving into a rubbish bin and finding everything it has ever loved! *Posted Friday 14th October at 21:58* [Comment . Like]

Katie Nikle likes the page **Every Social Interaction Can Be Made More Memorable Through The Introduction Of Swordplay.** [Like]

Madeline Cain Update #35, 365 Days of Fun: Pretend a friend is famous by following them around, taking photos, and shouting out their name. *Posted Saturday 15th October at 16:20* [Comment . Like]

> **Tim Gleeve** We really needed a bigger crowd for this to work better. *Posted Saturday 15th October at 16:25* [Comment . Like]

> **Madeline Cain** We probably should've given the 'limelight' to someone who looks like they could be famous. Claire for instance. *Posted Saturday 15th October at 16:29* [Comment . Like]

Tim Gleeve Owch. You wound me. *Posted Saturday 15th October at 16:33* [Comment . Like]

Madeline Cain I've owned about six-thousand bobby pins in my life. How many do I have left? Four. I have four. *Posted Saturday 15th October at 18:42* [Comment . Like]

Mike Cain I have achieved the impossible and made my sister look cool! I feel like I've been sucking God Vapours out of a vent in the ground and am now just an instrument for divine execution. *Posted Saturday 15th October at 20:10* [Comment . Like]

>   **Tim Gleeve** And have made yourself a highly inventive mortal enemy. She will find a way to humiliate you until the end of days. *sob* *Posted Saturday 15th October at 20:25* [Comment . Like]

>   **Mike Cain** Woose! We will see who is top dog in our family. Who will bomb, and who will be the bomb? *Posted Saturday 15th October at 20:36* [Comment . Like]

>   **Madeline Cain** Want to see a magic trick? Look into my eyes… Now think of a number between one and REVENGE. *Posted Saturday 15th October at 20:52* [Comment . Like]

Madeline Cain Brainstorming time! How will we punish Mike for his most recent transgression? All suggestions welcome as long as they fit on the spectrum between genital mauling by badger and immortalisation on Wikipedia as the person who has received the most wedgies in the history of the universe. You may get rewards. A swag, a gift basket, a finger painting by a five year old, a jar of bees, or whatever… *Posted Saturday 15th October at 22:22* [Comment . Like]

>   **Kathy Bloomingdale** Introduce Mike *to* a jar of bees? *Posted Saturday 15th October at 22:26* [Comment . Like]

>   **Tim Gleeve** Get him drunk and tattoo 'I love Carebears' on his

forehead? And a rainbow and unicorn on is butt cheeks? *Posted Saturday 15th October at 22:28* [Comment . Like]

Mike Cain Crown him King of Awesome Town. *Posted Saturday 15th October at 22:33* [Comment . Like]

Madeline Cain Kind of funny but also ruining my childhood memories of the Carebears. *Posted Saturday 15th October at 22:35* [Comment . Like]

Mike Cain Are you ignoring me? *Posted Saturday 15th October at 22:36* [Comment . Like]

Tim Gleeve I could set up a page declaring him the Mayor of Wedgieville? *Posted Saturday 15th October at 22:38* [Comment . Like]

Madeline Cain Might go part way to repaying your part in the whole fiasco. 'Might' being the key word here... *Posted Saturday 15th October at 22:39* [Comment . Like]

Mike Cain How is this any way to treat your beloved brother who got you on a plane to New York? *Posted Saturday 15th October at 22:40* [Comment . Like]

Kathy Bloomingdale You're not the first person to try that line this week. A pro tip, it didn't work last time. *Posted Saturday 15th October at 22:41* [Comment . Like]

Tim Gleeve I HAVE THE BEST IDEA! I'm texting it to you now. *Posted Saturday 15th October at 22:42* [Comment . Like]

Madeline Cain Let's do this. *Posted Saturday 15th October at 22:45* [Comment . Like]

Mike Cain Do what? What are you doing? *Posted Saturday 15th October at 22:47* [Comment . Like]

Tim Gleeve Who will bomb? And who will be the bomb? *Posted Saturday 15th October at 22:52* [Comment . Like]

Kathy Bloomingdale If I die on this return trip, all of you know that I love you. I bequeath my overprotective mother to Tim, and to dear Madeline I leave my hair accessories. May you never be bobby-pin-less again. *Posted Sunday 16th October at 04:33* [Comment . Like]

> **Tim Gleeve** Believe me when I say I have all of my fingers and toes crossed for your safe return. *Shudder.* *Posted Sunday 16th October at 08:53* [Comment . Like]

Kyle Traybna Officeworkssssssss. My Preciousssssss. *Posted Sunday 16th October at 10:23* [Comment . Like]

Isabelle Haigh Simple tips to gain my friendship: 1) Have a cat; 2) Show me pictures of your cat; 3) Invite me over to pet your cat; 4) Be a cat; 5) Cat. *Posted Sunday 16th October at 11:31* [Comment . Like]

Lulu Tanaki Me: Is it sexy the way tresses fall over the breasts in ringlets like curtains to a peep show? Hubby: Are you writing your children's book? *Posted Sunday 16th October at 14:40* [Comment . Like]

Mike Cain Ah my eyes! There's Glitter EVERYWHERE! Get it off, get it off!! *Posted Sunday 16th October at 17:56* [Comment . Like]

> **Madeline Cain** Some might say you've been glitter bombed. *Posted Sunday 16th October at 17:59* [Comment . Like]

> **Tim Gleeve** I understand you've just found a glitter stash in your baseball cap and socks. Wait til you find the rest... *Posted Sunday 16th October at 18:02* [Comment . Like]

> **Madeline Cain** Revenge high-five! *Posted Sunday 16th October at 18:03* [Comment . Like]

> **Tim Gleeve** *Smack!* *Posted Sunday 16th October at 18:04* [Comment . Like]

Mike Cain Why are these shiny harbingers of hell immune to the vacuum cleaner?? And showers?? Why!? *Posted Sunday 16th October at 18:12* [Comment . Like]

Tim Gleeve likes the page **Surprise Jazz Hands.** [Like]

Kathy Bloomingdale I'm alive! I'm alive! *Posted Monday 17th October at 11:11* [Comment . Like]

Madeline Cain She's alive! She's alive! Welcome home **Kathy**! *Posted Monday 17th October at 11:28* [Comment . Like]

Jack Fox likes the page **Who's Wearing The Pants In This Relationship? Well, Preferably No One.** [Like]

Madeline Cain Final Update, 365 Days of Fun: To celebrate the imminent departure of the 365 Day of Fun founder and creator, the delightful and irreplaceable Claire Holderness, we organised an early year twelve muck up day by upside-down-ing as many things in the school as we could without anyone noticing we were doing it. *Posted Wednesday 19th October at 16:30* [Comment . Like]

Tim Gleeve Upside Down Day was everything I ever imagined it to be and more! All that sneaking! All that confusion! *Posted Wednesday 19th October at 16:40* [Comment . Like]

Kathy Bloomingdale Claire is a ninja! A ninja I tell you! Not only did she turn every teachers' pen tin upside down but she managed to do it without any of the pens falling into a mess! *Posted Wednesday 19th October at 16:45* [Comment . Like]

Madeline Cain Ah the wonder of a piece of well-placed Blue-Tac at the bottom of the tin. You didn't do too bad yourself in the library. *Posted Wednesday 19th October at 16:48* [Comment . Like]

Kathy Bloomingdale Turning every book upside down in the shelf requires dedication, but I am committed to the cause… and

I may have had help from an Irish counterpart. *Posted Wednesday 19th October at 16:53* [Comment . Like]

Madeline Cain I don't know how I'm going to bear her leaving! *Posted Wednesday 19th October at 16:58* [Comment . Like]

Kathy Bloomingdale Said the kettle to the pot! *Posted Wednesday 19th October at 16:59* [Comment . Like]

Madeline Cain Today we farewelled our fellow co-conspirator, Claire, at the airport. She will be dearly missed and only reachable via the arcane novelty of the Australian and European postal services. Apparently technology gives her allergies. In exactly three months I too will be departing from this airport for New York where adventure waits! For this I owe her many heartfelt thanks. *Posted Saturday 22nd October at 13:13* [Comment . Like]

Kathy Bloomingdale You watch, she'll miss you so much she won't be able to help herself, tech allergies or no! *Posted Saturday 22nd October at 13:35* [Comment . Like]

Tim Gleeve I won't be that emotional when you leave, let me tell you. You're such a sap. Mike is still betting you won't get on that plane you know. *Posted Saturday 22nd October at 13:46* [Comment . Like]

Madeline Cain He's betting on the old me, not the new me. The new me has a new mantra. I am smart, I am curious, I am brave. *Posted Saturday 22nd October at 13:50* [Comment . Like]

Enjoyed Madeline Cain:
The Adventure Begins?

The Adventure Continues...

The Grand Adventures of Madeline Cain
(Book 2)

Available in all online book stores!

The problem with Facebook is, you can't fail at life in private.

Madeline Cain has made it! A New York City adventure and acceptance into a world famous photography school in Greenwich Village. What else could await an Australian in the big city but glamour, fun and kickass photo opportunities? All she needs is Facebook to brag to family and friends back home and she's set. Right? Right??

Not quite.

From the moment she's forced to make ends meet by accepting a job as a pizza delivery girl chaos becomes a close friend, much to the delight of her growing Facebook followers. As Madeline struggles not to embarrass herself in front of her hot (but taken) neighbour, Kevin, she must survive abusive umbrellas, deliveries to cross-dressing dwarfs, and completely unwarranted FBI questioning. Things move from the crazy to the ridiculous when she accidentally blackmails Kevin's millionaire girlfriend with photos of her cheating on him.

Does Madeline accept the bribe money she desperately needs or protect her budding relationship with Kevin the hottie?

Written as though you are reading Madeline's Facebook page, *The Grand Adventures of Madeline Cain* is a modern tale that will leave you in stitches.

Then Sign Up For The Newsletter!

Not only will you get a newsletter full of tales of adventure (I travel a *lot*) competitions, and my latest writing exploits, you'll get two bonus YA short-stories, *and* abusive umbrella message tones (?? oh, you'll understand soon).

Also, one lucky subscriber will be picked out of the hat to have a character named after them in my next novel. Congrats to lucky Claire Holderness who had a character named after her in this very novella!

Just sign up to my irregular author newsletter below (it may come to you monthly, maybe 6 monthly, it's a surprise for both of us! All you need to know is, I'm not into spam) to get your story gifts.

Sign up here! *http://www.cravenstories.com/books-and-more/freebies/reader-freebies/*

If You Enjoyed The Grand Adventures Of Madeline Cain, Please, Leave a Review Online!

Emily really appreciates every reader's support, and is stoked (pick the Aussie!) that you loved the book. If you could help her quit her day job to write more Madeline Cain novels by leaving a review at your favourite online retailer or Goodreads below she would love you forever! Please don't hesitate to email her either!

Review @ Goodreads: http://bit.ly/MCABGoodreads

Thank you! And see you at the next Adventure!

About The Author

Chocolate. Karaoke. Star Trek. Travel. Books. Puppies. Shaking what your Mama gave you. All of these are some of my favourite things. But when I meet someone, I want to know who they are, not what they like. I want to know what's their story? Why do they get up every morning? Other than, like, needing to have a pee.

Aherm, moving on.

For me, what rocks my world is showing daring creatives how to draw the curious down the rabbit hole with stories, how to use their tales to spark connection, understanding, and create belonging with a wonderland of their making.

Stories entered my DNA as a kid. They were what saved me from lonely lunch times with no friends when my family moved states and I was shoved into a new school mid-year, mid-puberty, mid-awkward-phase. They allowed me to escape to another world of adventure, of struggle (that wasn't mine), of empathy, perspective, and heroes who strived against the bullies, and again and again, picked themselves. Stories showed me how to adapt, to care, to trust myself. They understood me on a level I barely understood myself. I was such a voracious reader I started writing my own books when I was 12 because my favourite authors just couldn't keep up.

Stories were how I survived boredom. Boredom was how I ended up a Star Trek nerd. Every afternoon when I got home from school, my mother commandeered the TV to fuel her Star Trek addiction. The choice was be bored or be obsessed. You could say I was brain-washed a Trekkie and I have no regrets!

That's the only reason I can think of for how I ended up choosing to study Astrophysics. Two years in and something happened that I never in a million years expected. I hated it. I had no idea what else I would even do if I quit. I was good at it, sure, but every six months I would have a mini-break-down in my bedroom, the words of high-school teachers and parents going around and round my head – 'you're too smart for art.' If present me could time travel, I'd go back and slap them all up-side the head, with a loud, 'fuck that noise' for good measure.

How many times have you been told you 'should'? You should do this, you should do that, even though you know that box doesn't fit you?

What I didn't realise at the time was the reason I was so drawn to Star Trek wasn't the science, it was the adventure. A soap opera in space; people working together solving problems, falling in love, and shooting phasers! This was the root of my unhappiness; I was suppressing the biggest part of myself. I didn't want knowledge for the sake of knowledge, I want to create things that connected people. And the way that excited me, that lit a fire in my belly to create that connection, was by creating and sharing stories. Fictional preferably, with a hint of magic, a dash of quirky, and a sneaky side of truth.

I wish I could tell you that when I set my sights on career as storyteller, I shook off that 'should' energy. I did not. While I devoured dozens of courses on writing, publishing, marketing, editing and eBooks, and learnt one of the most important lessons of my life – that what you create alone will never be as good as what you'll create together with the feedback of professionals who aren't you and see your blind spots – I was still doing all the things you should. You should send your novels to traditional publishers, you should write short stories to get a name for yourself, you should have a 'very' professional website where you're 'very serious' and therefore 'competent', as confirmed by your head shot which makes you look like you have sat on a cactus.

I waited a really long time for someone to pick me. And I was lonely, so very very lonely. When a boy who already had a 3-book deal with a major publisher got the only writing grant available in the state to writers under 30, something finally snapped for me. I was sick of waiting; it was time to choose myself. I couldn't be rejected if I was the one creating the thing, right?

It was when I took the conscious decision to step off the beaten path that things changed for me. I created my own opportunities, but in a way that no one else was doing at the time – I created them so that I was making and creating WITH someone else. The power of collaboration runs through everything I do now, from the very first writing and publishing project I created in my little city of Adelaide, which spiralled into a 5-year international endeavour that would turn into the award-winning storytelling app, Story City, and lift up over 300 storytellers across half a dozen creative industries.

In creating my own opportunities, in making things like Story City, my novels, my branding work, I realised I made a place where I belonged, and where hundreds and thousands of others realised they belonged.

The success that I have had today is due largely to the power of story. Of how stories allow you to be understood for you, and to connect beyond yourself. I've won awards, presented hundreds of hours of storytelling workshops internationally, published 6 books, edited and/or published dozens of authors, I am a global entrepreneur of an app that helps you explore and connect to a city and the stories of its people, and I'm part of a 6 person team that brands a handful of high-flying femmpreneurs every year.

While much of that has been because of hard work, talent, and practice, the truth of the matter is I have gotten this far because I have chosen to make things together, rather than alone. To hone my understanding, skills and stories, with outside eyes, because through collaboration I make far more impact than I ever would on my own.

So I say to you pick yourself, don't wait for others to pick you. But also pick doing it together, rather than doing it alone.

Find your people. Band together. And you will make great things.

With This Book You Also Get A Free Ebook Copy!

Just email emily@cravenstories.com with the following to prove your purchase:

- A photo of yourself holding the book PLUS;
- A photo of your name written in pen on the copyright page;
- Mention where you bought the book from.
- What format you would like the book in: .epub (iPad, Kobo, Nook etc), .mobi (Kindle/Amazon) or PDF.

Once Emily receives your email she will personally email you back your e-book copy. She's only human, so give her a couple of days to get to your email. Thank you once again for purchasing the book!

Contact Emily Online

Facebook: *http://www.facebook.com/EmilyCravenAuthor*

Website (bookmark me!): *http://www.cravenstories.com*

Twitter: *@cravenstories*

Instagram: *@imagesforjoy*

My Email: emily (at) cravenstories (dot) com

www.ingramcontent.com/pod-product-compliance
Lightning Source LLC
Chambersburg PA
CBHW070024120726
47909CB00003B/1053